# Mastering Defense: The Art and Science of Preventing Goals in Soccer

## Strategy, Resilience, Perseverance, and the Unsung Heroes of Soccer

*"Attack wins you games, Defense wins you titles."*
*- Sir Alex Ferguson*

## KEVIN LE DOUX

# *Foreword*

Mastering Defense: The Art and Science of Preventing Goals in Soccer, by Kevin Le Doux, also known in many soccer circles as Coach K, is an absolute game-changer. This book offers a comprehensive insider's look into the soul of soccer's most unsung heroes—the defenders. From the opening page, Le Doux takes readers on a journey through the intricate world of defending, transforming the art of stopping goals into a compelling narrative of strategy, skill, mental resilience, and perseverance.

What makes this book truly unique is how it speaks to players and fans alike, unraveling the complexities of defensive play with a clarity that resonates at every level. Le Doux's expertise as a coach and former player is evident; he doesn't just teach techniques—he teaches a mentality, a way of thinking and being on the field that will inspire defenders and captivate all who admire the game. With memorable anecdotes, humor, and real-world examples, he connects readers to the thrill, precision, and challenges defenders face, often in the critical moments of the match.

As Nick Zlatar, former East Regional Coach for the United States Soccer Federation (USSF), aptly states, "Kevin Le Doux helps the reader attain a deeper understanding of the great game of soccer and the art of defending." This endorsement highlights the profound impact of Le Doux's insights and the unique value this book provides to players, coaches, and enthusiasts.

In each chapter, Le Doux covers every conceivable aspect of defense, from mental preparation and teamwork to the split-second decision-making that defines the game's best defenders. Illustrated with diagrams and supported by reflective prompts, this book is not only instructional but deeply engaging, giving readers the tools they need to elevate their game.

Whether you're an aspiring player, a seasoned coach, or a fan wanting to deepen your appreciation for soccer, Mastering Defense is a must-read. Kevin Le Doux has created more than a manual—he's written a tribute to the heart and science of defending that will undoubtedly stand as a cornerstone in soccer literature for years to come. Prepare to dive in, learn, and see soccer through the eyes of those who keep the dream alive, one brilliant defensive play at a time.

## *About The Author*

Kevin Le Doux's journey from Georgetown, Guyana, to the United States is a testament to perseverance, resilience, passion, and an enduring love for soccer. Born to hardworking parents Ernest and Norma, Kevin grew up in a close-knit family, learning early the values of dedication and sacrifice. As the eldest sibling, he felt a deep sense of responsibility, supporting his family through his early role as an Audit Clerk in Guyana's Transport and Harbors Head Office. In 1979, he made the life-changing decision to migrate to the United States, seeking opportunities to provide a better future for his loved ones.

Adapting to life in the fast-paced landscape of Brooklyn, New York, was no easy feat. Initially overwhelmed by the towering buildings and relentless pace, Kevin put soccer aside temporarily to focus on adjusting to his new environment. He took on work as an Account Clerk. He worked his way up the ladder to become the Assistant Director of Materials Management at the State University of New York Health Science Center at Brooklyn, balancing his professional responsibilities with his studies. After briefly pursuing a degree in Architecture at Pratt Institute, he discovered a new path at Brooklyn College, ultimately earning a Bachelor of Science degree in Business Management and Finance in 1992.

Soccer, however, remained Kevin's lifelong passion and his true calling. Over five decades, he's built an extraordinary career as a semi-professional player, coach, and referee, blending his rich playing experience with an unrelenting drive to develop others. In the mid-1970s, Kevin was selected to represent the Guyanese National Team, though life's responsibilities led him to take another path. Yet, in 1996, he proudly represented Guyana in the Caribbean Cup Soccer tournament, a defining moment in his career.

In March 1996, Kevin, alongside Dr. Dexter Hazlewood—a fellow Guyanese and now author— founded the Guyanese North American Soccer Association (GNASA). Their mission was to assist the GFF in fostering the development of football in Guyana by harnessing the talents of footballers scattered throughout the diaspora and facilitating their training for integration into the GFF's junior and senior national teams. Despite their passion, commitment, and some successes, challenges led to its dissolution in 2004. However, this setback did not diminish Kevin's resolve to contribute to the sport he loves. That same year, Kevin participated in another defining moment of his career by conducting a coaching clinic alongside George Weah, the first African and non-European player to win the

Ballon d'Or (1995) after the award was expanded to include the best footballer globally. George Weah, who is now the President of Liberia, brought his wealth of experience and inspiration to the event, offering Kevin an invaluable opportunity to exchange ideas and further refine his coaching approach.

Kevin's accomplishments as a coach and mentor are equally impressive. Holding National Coaching licensure from the United States Soccer Federation and a series of La Liga Formation Methodology certifications, he has distinguished himself among his peers. In 2020, he became one of only two Guyanese among the very first eighteen coaches in the United States to complete US Club Soccer's inaugural La Liga Formation Methodology certification conferred in Madrid, Spain. This experience not only honed his skills but offered him the distinct pleasure of meeting soccer luminaries like Unai Emery, then-manager of Paris Saint-Germain, and the legendary Raúl González. Their insights, generously shared as part of the course, have stayed with Kevin, inspiring his coaching philosophy and approach. Furthermore, these certifications, along with the grooming and mentorship of Coaches Desmond Morgan and Nick Zlatar, have been instrumental in Kevin's growth as a successful coach, shaping his ability to inspire and uplift athletes to new levels of achievement.

In July 2024, Kevin was selected as part of the Guyana Football Federation's coaching staff to identify talented players for Youth National Representation. This prestigious role underscores Kevin's lifelong commitment to fostering soccer talent and his dedication to contributing to the sport on an international level.

Kevin's dedication to soccer has profoundly impacted his community. Through coaching young players, organizing local tournaments, and supporting outreach initiatives such as the Economic Opportunity Council of Suffolk, Inc., he has cultivated talent and fostered unity among soccer enthusiasts. During his spare time, Kevin participates in "Charity Games" to help raise funds for notable causes, including The American Cancer Society, the fallen heroes of the 106 ANG Rescue Wing of Long Island, the Nine Eleven Veterans of Long Island, and The Lighthouse Missions of Long Island. His efforts have made the game more accessible and enjoyable, inspiring future generations to embrace and excel both in soccer and life. His unique approach to coaching is holistic, integrating skills from Spring Forest QiGong to enhance players' focus and self-awareness on and off the field.

One of Kevin's proudest moments as a mentor came in 2022, when a former student, JB, drove across states to introduce Kevin to his girlfriend, citing the profound impact Kevin had on his life. Their bond was further honored when JB invited Kevin to his wedding in Atlanta two years later—a testament to Kevin's influence far beyond the field.

In January 2024, Kevin reconnected with Dr. Hazlewood and became a Senior Consultant for Elite Consultants EC, LLC. This independent company is dedicated to the development of football wherever it is played and for any country in need of its expertise. Kevin's journey—from co-founding GNASA to joining EC, LLC—reflects his unwavering determination to advance football development, regardless of challenges or setbacks.

Today, Kevin continues to inspire athletes, coaches, and readers through his commitment to fostering perseverance, resilience, adaptability, teamwork, and personal growth. His favorite guiding principle, from mentor Dr. Wayne Dyer, echoes throughout his teachings: "By believing in that which does not exist, we create it. That which is non-existent was not sufficiently desired."

For Kevin, this philosophy extends beyond belief; it underscores the importance of coupling vision with action to bring aspirations to life, demonstrating that determination and effort are essential to transforming dreams into reality.

# Contents

# List of Chapters

**Chapter 1: Developing a Winning Mentality in Defense**
The importance of mental preparation, focus, resilience, and perseverance in becoming a top defender. Includes visualization techniques, goal-setting, and reflective prompts.

**Chapter 2: Mastering Defensive Positioning and Tactics**
Detailed exploration of positioning strategies, including zonal marking, man-marking, and the offside trap.
Features tactical diagrams and practical examples.

**Chapter 3: Tackling and Interceptions— The Art of Winning the Ball**
Techniques for executing clean tackles and smart interceptions. Emphasizes timing, discipline, and anticipation with
real-life anecdotes.

**Chapter 4: Working with the Goalkeeper and Defensive Chemistry**
Building trust and communication between defenders and goalkeepers. Covers the principles of defensive unity, including pressure, cover, balance, and compactness.

**Chapter 5: Defending Set Pieces— Mastering High-Pressure Moments**
Strategies for corners, free kicks, and other set-piece scenarios. Discusses marking systems and techniques for maintaining focus under pressure.

**Chapter 6: Possession and Transitions— The Power of Scanning and Turning Defense into Attack**
How defenders can regain and retain possession while transitioning to attack.
Highlights the role of scanning and quick decision-making.

**Chapter 7: Defensive Leadership and Communication —The Voice That Commands**
The role of communication and leadership in organizing the backline and guiding the team.
Includes practical tips for vocal clarity and mental composure.

**Chapter 8: Defensive Resilience and Adaptability**
Adapting to tactical changes, injuries, and high-pressure moments. Focuses on developing resilience and staying composed under adversity.

**Chapter 9: Controlling the Game from the Backlin— Dictating the Tempo and Pacing the Match**
How defenders influence the flow of play by controlling the tempo and maintaining composure.
Discusses strategies for managing transitions and imposing defensive dominance.

**Chapter 10: The Complete Defender—Mastering the Art and Science of Preventing Goals**
A holistic guide to becoming a well-rounded defender. Integrates mental, physical, and tactical aspects for mastering the craft of preventing goals.

# *Acknowledgments*

This book is a culmination of countless experiences and the profound impact of the people who have supported me along the way.

To my fellow students and coaches, especially Desmond Morgan and Nick Zlatar—you have shaped my coaching philosophy in ways I could never have imagined. The insights, dedication, and perspectives of my coaches have continuously inspired me to reach new heights in the beautiful game.

To Dr. Dexter Hazlewood, my childhood best friend, teammate, unwavering supporter, and business partner. Dexter, thank you for your relentless encouragement critical feedback, and for believing in this project even when I hesitated. Ironically, while I've focused on the art of defending, you've ventured into the thrill of scoring, recently publishing your book, The Anatomy of Goal Scoring in Soccer. Sharing the field as teammates alongside you remains one of my most cherished experiences, and seeing how we've both carried that love for the game into new arenas deepens my appreciation for this journey. Beyond that, your tireless efforts to help me bring this book to print with your collaboration have been nothing short of exemplary.

To Armel Sejour, thank you for the camaraderie and understanding we shared as teammates. Playing alongside you was a privilege and remains a cherished memory. Your contributions to this journey remind me of the profound impact of teamwork, both in soccer and in life.

To Christopher Michael Duncan, becoming a member of your Magnetic Mind Master Class and reading your books—*You're Not Broken and The Superconscious Path*—was one of the best decisions and investments I have ever made. Your teachings empowered me to "start creating the life I love and living my true nature and purpose,"—one of which was writing this book. Thank you for being a catalyst in helping me realize this dream.

To Master Chunyi Lin, your teachings have profoundly shaped my approach to coaching and life. As your student, learning Spring Forest QiGong has been transformative, enabling me to integrate its principles to enhance players' focus and self-awareness both on and off the field.

Your wisdom has been a guiding light in helping me blend mindfulness with athletic performance. Thank you for your invaluable influence.

To Cameron Germano, your relentless strength and hours of hard work as the graphic designer responsible for making this book come to life for the reader are astounding and deeply appreciated. Thank you.

To Alexander Rohman of Time Capital, a true friend and generous soul—your incredible support, particularly in granting me access to your staff and copy machine, was instrumental in getting this book to print. Your kindness and willingness to assist made a world of difference in this journey. Thank you for playing such a vital role in bringing this dream to fruition.

To Dimitri Gibbs, your extraordinary creativity and vision transformed the concept of my book cover into a masterpiece that surpassed even my highest expectations. Your ability to capture the essence of my vision and bring it to life with such precision and artistry is a testament to your remarkable talent. Thank you for your dedication and for playing such a pivotal role in shaping this book's identity. Your work will forever be a source of pride and inspiration for me.

To those that I have not singled out personally and who have contributed in some form or another, please note that you are very much appreciated and not forgotten. Your impact, whether seen or unseen, has been instrumental in bringing this project to life.

Thank you for being part of this incredible journey.

I dedicate this book to the memory of my beloved mother, Norma, and my siblings, Gavin and Allison.

Though you have moved on from this earthly realm, your love remains a guiding presence in my life. To my father, Ernest, and my siblings Roger, Sean, and Stacey—your silent yet unwavering love has been a source of strength that I have cherished every step of the way.

"To Norma, my beloved wife — your love, care, and unwavering support have been the heartbeat behind this journey. You were my biggest supporter. Through every triumph and every trial, you stood by me with quiet strength and endless patience. You shared the long nights, the sacrifices, and the moments of doubt, always believing in my dream even when the road was uncertain. From the early days of my playing career to the completion of this book, you gave me courage, peace, and purpose. I will forever be grateful for the years we walked together side by side, for your steadfast faith in me, and for the light you brought to my path."

And to my daughters, Tiffani and Teresalyn, "T-Lyn"—you are my heart, my inspiration, and my guiding light. Your love gives meaning to every goal I pursue, on and off the field. I am especially grateful for the time and effort you devoted to reviewing the manuscript and providing thoughtful feedback. Your insights not only enriched this work but also reminded me of how fortunate I am to have you both by my side. This book reflects not just my journey but the shared love, laughter, and commitment we bring to everything we undertake as a family.

# *Preface*

Soccer is a game of contrasts: triumph and heartbreak, speed and patience, strength and finesse. Yet, at the heart of every victory lies a constant—defense. Defense is the backbone, the element that holds it all together, turning the impossible into reality. It's about more than stopping a goal; it's about anticipation, adaptation, and using every ounce of focus to read the game. And these qualities extend far beyond the field. They are life skills—skills that build resilience, sharpen instincts, and teach us to stay steady under pressure.

*Mastering Defense: The Art and Science of Preventing Goals in Soccer* is a tribute to the defenders, those unsung heroes whose contributions are often overshadowed by the glitz and glory of goals. These players shape the game in ways most spectators never see, bringing artistry to defending that demands intelligence, grit, and dedication. Just as defense forms a foundation for success on the field, it can also serve as a guide for navigating life's challenges.
Like great defenders, we all face moments when a single decision, a quick adjustment, or a surge of inner strength can alter our course.

In these pages, you'll discover more than tactics and strategies—you'll uncover the mindset that drives a defender to rise to the occasion, time and time again. Each chapter, drawing from the wisdom of iconic players, memorable matches, and real-life humor, explores how principles like patience, adaptability, and resilience cultivate an unbreakable mindset both on and off the field. I've blended practical guidance with life lessons, memorable examples, and reflective prompts, encouraging you to view defending as both a skill and a philosophy.

For me, writing this book has been about sharing these life-shaping lessons as much as the technical strategies that form a defender's arsenal. As you read, I hope you'll find insights that elevate not only your game but also your journey beyond soccer. Embrace this opportunity to learn, grow, and see defense—on the field and in life—as a powerful, purposeful stance.

This book is an invitation to embody the spirit of defense: steadfast, proactive, and ever-ready. Join me on this journey into the art of defending as we celebrate what it means to be both a player on the field and a champion of resilience in life.

# *Introduction: The Defensive Playbook*

In the world of soccer, goals often steal the headlines, but behind every great victory stands an unsung hero: the defender. While strikers revel in the glory of scoring, it's the defensive wall that endures, holding strong and building the foundation on which championships are won. When executed with precision, defending is more than just stopping goals—it transforms into a strategic art that demands intelligence, positioning, and mental strength.

Defense is the quiet hero of soccer, the backbone that lets brilliance thrive. Consider this: a perfectly timed tackle, a subtle interception, or the foresight to cut off a pass before it happens— these moments often go unnoticed, yet they are the true turning points in any game. A split-second decision by a defender can be the difference between triumph and defeat. Defensive play is a game of anticipation, awareness, and discipline, where every move is calculated and every step deliberate.

This book goes beyond the clichés of "stopping the ball" and into the intricate science of defending—a craft that fuses athleticism with tactical intelligence. You'll journey through the techniques, strategies, and mental frameworks that separate the elite defender from the rest.

Along the way, you'll learn from legends who mastered the art of defense and carved their paths in soccer history, building personal playbooks that defined their careers. By immersing yourself in these lessons, you'll not only develop the skills to play defense but to command it.

Whether you're an aspiring player or a seasoned defender looking to elevate your game, this book is your blueprint.
Here, you'll discover how to master the principles of defense, understand the chemistry of a cohesive defensive unit, and transform into a dominant force on the field.

Defense is more than an act of resistance—it's a statement of control, precision, and anticipation. Welcome to the art and science of defense, where every move you make lays the foundation for greatness.

# CHAPTER 1: Developing a Winning Mentality in Defense

***Picture This***: It's the 89th minute of a critical match. Your team is leading 1–0, but the opposing team is pressing hard. The ball moves quickly between their forwards, looking for an opening. Everything hinges on this moment. You read the play, anticipate the pass, step in to intercept—and just like that, the attack is over. This is what the right mentality allows you to do: stay calm, make the right decisions, and save the game in critical moments. Isn't this what life is all about?

**Introduction: The Mental Game in Defense**

Defending in soccer is not just about strength, tackling, or positioning—it's about mastering the mental game. Before you can ***outmaneuver an opponent or clear a ball off the line, you must first cultivate the right*** mindset. Becoming an elite defender requires sharp mental preparation, discipline, and resilience.

As Chunyi Lin, an internationally renowned QiGong Master and Holistic Healer, insightfully states in Born a Healer, "Everything you do and think creates a ripple in the energy of the universe. Be mindful of your actions and intentions—they are seeds of change." This concept underscores the foundation of great defending: intentionality.

Whether it's visualizing a critical interception or focusing on staying composed during pressure-packed moments, your thoughts shape your actions and, ultimately, your performance.

With this in mind, defenders can harness intentionality by integrating specific mental strategies, such as visualization techniques and focused breathing exercises, to enhance their composure and decision-making on the pitch.

*Mastering Defense: The Art and Science of Preventing Goals* begins here—with the brainwork that separates the good from the great.

As Coach Nick Zlatar puts it, "Every great defender has a story, a reason they became who they are. It's often about finding the right mix of skill, mindset, and a bit of an unteachable quality— something intangible that you can't put into words but can see in their play."

And he's absolutely right. Being an exceptional defender goes beyond drills and tactical training—it's about developing a unique mentality, one that combines experience, inner grit, and an almost instinctive sense of timing.

**The Importance of Mental Preparation**

Every top defender understands that preparation for a game starts long before stepping onto the pitch. Sir Alex Ferguson once said, "Winning matches is about preparation," and the same goes for defending.

A defender's readiness involves more than just physical conditioning; it's about mental discipline, anticipation, and focus. Whether it's Beckenbauer, van Dijk, or Maldini, the mental game is what sets these players apart.

**Visual Aid 2: Key Aspects of Mental Focus for Defenders**

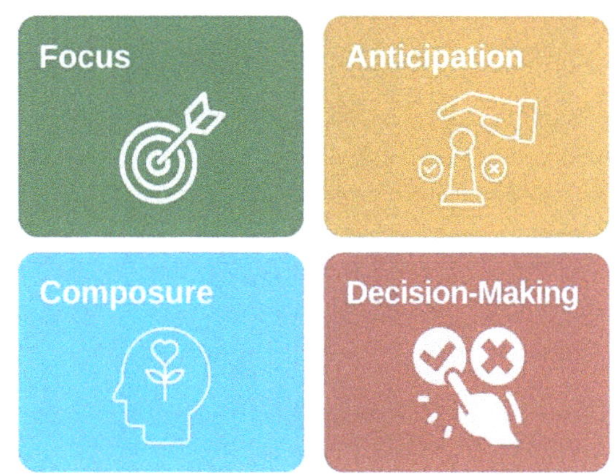


## Visualization: See Success before It Happens

Before the whistle blows, elite defenders engage in visualization. This technique allows players to mentally rehearse their performance, envisioning themselves reading the game, anticipating moves, and executing perfect tackles. This approach is rooted in the idea that mental preparation creates the conditions for external success.

Christopher Duncan, an author, a personal development coach, and a noted expert on personal structure, once said, "You are not going to get results externally unless you can truly see yourself being or having achieved it internally first." He emphasizes, "You must be it to get it!" Visualizing in your mind the actions, the feelings, and the outcomes you seek—then following through with action—is a powerful method of transformation. It aligns perfectly with Chunyi Lin's principle from *Born a Healer*: "Everything you do and think creates a ripple in the energy of the universe. Be mindful of your actions and intentions—they are seeds of change." Together, these perspectives highlight how visualization combines belief and intention, setting the stage for success.

Carles Puyol, the legendary Barcelona captain, epitomized this principle on the pitch. Known for his unyielding commitment and focus, Puyol would often describe how he mentally prepared for games by envisioning scenarios—blocking shots, intercepting passes, or leading his teammates in critical moments. Puyol himself said, "When you visualize yourself performing well, your confidence grows. You see the challenges before they happen, and you're ready." His approach reflects the essence of visualization: anticipating challenges and preparing to conquer them.

To build a similar habit, players can begin incorporating visualization into their training sessions. Spend a few minutes before each session mentally rehearsing key defensive maneuvers—whether it's anticipating an interception, executing a clean tackle, or maintaining composure under pressure. Just as Puyol did, use this practice to enhance focus, align your intentions with your actions, and prepare yourself to lead with confidence when it matters most.

**Visual Aid 3: The Visualization Process for Defenders**



**Setting Clear, Achievable Goals**

Defenders, like all athletes, need a roadmap to success. Setting personal and team goals helps focus efforts and directs energy where it's needed most. Cristiano Ronaldo once said, "If you don't believe you are the best, then you will never achieve all that you are capable of."

While defenders may not have the same goal-scoring ambitions, setting clear, defined goals is critical.

Short-term goals might include improving defensive positioning, achieving a specific number of successful tackles or interceptions in a match, or maintaining consistent communication with teammates during a game. These immediate objectives help players stay focused on specific aspects of their performance.

Long-term goals could involve becoming a team leader in defensive statistics over a season, mastering zonal and man-marking systems, or earning recognition for defensive consistency at a higher level of competition. These ambitions provide a broader sense of purpose and direction, ensuring continuous growth over time.

**Visual Aid 4: Defender's Goal-Setting**



By setting both short-term and long-term goals, defenders create a clear path to success—one that allows them to measure progress, stay motivated, and continually improve their game.

**Mastering the Mental Side of Resilience**

Resilience in defense is the unshakable backbone of a great player. Mistakes are inevitable in soccer, as in life. What defines an elite defender is not avoiding errors but how they respond to them. Resilience is about maintaining composure and staying mentally in the game after a missed clearance, a tackle, or a momentary lapse in focus.
It is the ability to reset quickly, re-center, and approach the next challenge with renewed determination.

To guide you on this journey, let me share a mantra—a personal and transformative tool that will act as a modern-day philosopher's stone throughout this book:

*"If my mind can conceive it, and my heart believe it, then I CAN achieve it!!!

Because I am talented, gifted, and strong.

Today as always, I will do my best in all things.
The results will follow because:

- I am focused

- I am Mentally tough

- I am Confident

- I am Well prepared

- I am Resilient

- I am Persistent

- I'm in the BEAST mode!!!!"*

The "*Philosopher's Stone.*" I first learnt of this term from the book, The Superconscious Path by Christopher Michael Duncan. Historically, the philosopher's stone is a legendary substance in alchemy, believed to transform base metals into gold and grant immortality. Symbolically, it represents personal transformation, the pursuit of excellence, and the ability to overcome challenges.

In this context, the mantra serves as your philosopher's stone—a tool to transform your mindset, fortify your resilience, and unlock your potential both on and off the field.

**Real-Life Application**

Consider a defender who concedes an own goal—arguably one of the toughest moments to overcome emotionally during a match. A resilient player would acknowledge the mistake, adjust their focus, and commit to making impactful contributions for the remainder of the game.

Whether through a critical interception, a perfectly timed tackle, or inspiring communication with teammates, resilience enables a defender to turn a moment of failure into fuel for future success.

**Practical Strategies for Building Resilience:**

**Reframe Mistakes as Learning Opportunities**

Every error holds a lesson. Reflect on what went wrong and determine how to approach similar situations differently in the future.

**Develop a Reset Routine**

After a mistake, take a deep breath, reset your focus, and visualize success in your next action. This mental pause helps clear negative emotions and prepares you to respond constructively.

**Foster a Growth Mindset**

As psychologist Carol Dweck emphasizes, viewing challenges as opportunities to grow strengthens resilience. In defense, this mindset keeps players proactive and adaptable in high-pressure situations.

For instance, imagine a scenario where a defender misjudges an opponent's run, leading to a dangerous counterattack. Instead of dwelling on the mistake, a defender with a growth mindset sees it as a learning moment—quickly analyzing what went wrong and making adjustments to prevent it from happening again.

This adaptability could involve improving communication with teammates, refining positioning, or anticipating the opponent's next move
more effectively.
By embracing challenges and focusing on continuous improvement, defenders can not only recover from setbacks but also elevate their overall performance.

**Stay Grounded Through Team Support**

Resilient players are also great teammates. Building trust with your defensive line allows you to rely on collective strength and communication to bounce back from setbacks.

Adding these tools to your mental arsenal transforms resilience from a trait into a skill—one that becomes second nature over time.

Resilience in defense isn't just about holding strong in the game; it's about bouncing back from mistakes. Defensive resilience is the grit and determination to keep pushing, even after an error. It's about focusing forward and maintaining composure, knowing each game will present new challenges.

**Real-Life Example**

Gary Cahill's resilience was on full display in the 2012 Champions League semi-final when Chelsea was down a player against Barcelona. Chelsea was under siege, yet Cahill's resilience kept them calm, clearing attack after attack and eventually helping Chelsea win a place in the final.

**Humor Break**

*"Sometimes, defenders say they're allergic to clean sheets—they just can't seem to hold onto one. But in reality, every clean sheet feels like scoring a hat-trick!" This underscores the importance of maintaining a clean sheet by preventing an opponent from scoring.*

**The Role of Perseverance: The Heartbeat of a Defender's Mentality**

While resilience equips defenders to bounce back from mistakes or setbacks, perseverance is what keeps them pushing forward in the face of relentless challenges. It's the inner drive that powers defenders through moments of exhaustion, sustained pressure, or seemingly unwinnable situations. Perseverance transforms effort into an enduring force, ensuring defenders stay engaged and committed until the final whistle.

Legendary center-back Franco Baresi exemplified this trait during the 1994 FIFA World Cup final. Playing through immense fatigue and pain, he refused to let up, leading Italy's defense against Brazil with unwavering determination. Though the match ended in heartbreak during penalties, Baresi's perseverance inspired his teammates and cemented his place as a symbol of defensive grit.

For defenders, perseverance means:

- Chasing down every ball, even in the dying minutes of a match.

- Maintaining focus and effort when the team is under constant attack.

- Continuously refining skills, regardless of setbacks or slow progress.

**Practical Tips to Cultivate Perseverance:**

1. Set Small, Actionable Goals: Focus on winning your next challenge or staying alert for the next defensive play, breaking big tasks into manageable actions.

2. Find Inspiration in Others: Study players known for their never-give-up attitude to learn how they approach tough situations.

3. Practice Staying Mentally Present: Use breathing exercises or mantras like "One more step" to stay locked in during physically or emotionally draining moments.

Together with resilience, perseverance ensures defenders not only recover from setbacks but also endure and thrive under sustained adversity. As Coach Nick Zlatar said, *"Defenders succeed not just by recovering from failure but by refusing to stop trying."*

**Conclusion: Building a Defender's Mental Fortress**

Mastering the mental side of defense is where the foundation for success begins. As we've explored in this chapter, defending is not just about physicality or sheer athleticism—it's about cultivating the mental resilience and sharpness that allows you to anticipate, stay composed, and make intelligent decisions under pressure.

The impact of mental preparation extends beyond individual performance; it influences the entire team's success and cohesion. A composed and mentally prepared defender instills confidence in their teammates, creating a ripple effect that boosts communication, trust, and unity across the pitch. When defenders anticipate threats and maintain composure, they set the tone for the team's defensive organization and foster a collective belief that challenges can be met with focus and resilience.

The greatest defenders—like Virgil van Dijk, Paolo Maldini, and Franz Beckenbauer—have shown us that it's the mind that sets them apart from the rest. Their mental fortitude didn't just elevate their own game; it made those around them better, turning individual brilliance into cohesive team success.

Visualization, mental discipline, and goal-setting are essential tools in shaping this winning mentality. When you approach each game with clear focus and intention, as Dr. Wayne Dyer emphasized, your reality on the field changes. Mental preparation ensures that you're ready not only for the physical demands of the game but also for the mental battles that arise in moments of chaos.

## Visual Aid 5: Defensive Resilience and Perseverance in Action

**Mental Toughness beyond the Pitch**

The winning mentality required in defense mirrors the challenges we face in life. Just as defenders rely on focus, preparation, resilience, and perseverance to shut down attacks, these same qualities are invaluable off the field.

- ***Anticipation and Adaptability***: On the pitch, defenders practice reading the game by analyzing opponents' movements, predicting plays, and adjusting their positioning to stay one step ahead. Similarly, in real-life scenarios—whether managing a career shift, solving problems, or navigating personal relationships—this ability to anticipate challenges and adapt to evolving situations often determines success. For example, just as a defender learns to interpret subtle cues like an attacker's body language or passing patterns, individuals can develop a similar awareness by observing patterns and cues in their own environments, enabling them to respond proactively and effectively.

- ***Goal-Setting for Growth***: Defenders set achievable goals to measure and improve performance.
  Similarly, setting clear goals in life helps channel effort, build momentum, and achieve lasting results.

- ***Resilience after Mistakes***: Life, like soccer, is filled with moments of imperfection. Learning to recover quickly, maintain composure, and grow from mistakes is crucial to overcoming adversity.

- ***Perseverance through Challenges***: Perseverance fuels the determination to keep striving when the path forward seems difficult or uncertain. It ensures effort remains consistent, even during tough times, leading to personal growth and long-term success. For example, legendary defender Vincent Kompany overcame multiple career-threatening injuries through sheer perseverance, returning each time with an unwavering commitment to his team and craft. His journey serves as a powerful reminder that setbacks are not the end but an opportunity to come back stronger. As Kompany once said, *"The road to success is never straight, but persistence turns obstacles into stepping stones."*

The lessons from developing a defender's mentality—preparation, visualization, resilience, and perseverance—extend far beyond the game. They empower us to face life's challenges with confidence, purpose, and determination, just as elite defenders do when protecting their goals.

Whether on the pitch or in daily life, building this mental fortress equips us to thrive in any high-pressure moment.

**Memorable Takeaways (with Reflective Prompts)**

**Resilience Turns Mistakes Into Opportunities**

Great defenders don't dwell on errors; they learn and bounce back stronger. Resilience means staying composed, making adjustments, and responding positively after setbacks.

*Reflective Prompt*: Think of a game where a mistake challenged your focus. How did you recover, and what steps can you take to build even stronger resilience in future matches?

**Perseverance Sustains Effort through Challenges**

Perseverance drives defenders to keep striving even when faced with fatigue, pressure, or adversity. It ensures continuous effort and commitment, especially in the toughest moments.

*Reflective Prompt*: Recall a time when you felt exhausted or under constant pressure during a match but kept pushing forward.
What motivated you to persist, and how can you strengthen this determination in future games?

**Preparation Is the Foundation of Success**

Elite defenders begin preparing long before the match starts. Mental preparation through visualization and setting clear goals sharpens instincts and builds confidence.

*Reflective Prompt*: Recall a time when mental preparation influenced your performance. How can you refine your pre-match routine to enhance your focus and readiness?

## Visualization Sharpens Anticipation

Envisioning critical moments—reading an attacker's move, timing a tackle, or clearing a dangerous cross—helps defenders anticipate the game and execute with precision.

*Reflective Prompt:* Reflect on a time when you anticipated a play and turned it into a key defensive moment. How can you use visualization to improve this skill?

## Goal-Setting Drives Improvement

Setting specific, measurable goals, such as winning aerial duels or blocking shots, creates focus and motivation. These small objectives add up to a bigger impact on the game.

*Reflective Prompt:* Identify a recent defensive goal you set for yourself. How did it affect your performance, and what new goals can you pursue to elevate your game further?

## Focus and Adaptability Are Game-Changers

In high-pressure moments, staying mentally sharp is crucial. A focused defender reacts calmly to evolving situations and adapts to the unpredictable flow of the game.

*Reflective Prompt:* Think of a match where focus helped you handle a chaotic moment on the field. How can you improve your ability to stay locked in during intense situations?

These takeaways reinforce the mindset of an elite defender, helping players grow both on and off the pitch. Reflecting on these concepts will not only sharpen your defensive skills but also equip you with valuable life lessons.

## Summary and Bread Crumbs for Future Chapters

In this chapter, we laid the groundwork for developing a winning mentality in defense, focusing on the mental preparation required to excel on the field. We explored the importance of visualization, goal-setting, and mental resilience, all of which set the stage for mastering the art of defending. However, mental preparation is only the first step in becoming an elite defender. Take a moment to reflect on how these principles can apply to your own matches and consider how adopting them, could elevate your game to the next level.

In the next chapter, we will dive deeper into defensive positioning and tactics. You'll learn how the mental game integrates with physical positioning—how being in the right place at the right time is critical to shutting down attacks and maintaining defensive stability. We'll explore how great defenders, from Franz Beckenbauer to Virgil van Dijk, use their intelligence and awareness to dominate the field and outthink their opponents.

# CHAPTER 2: *Mastering Defensive Positioning and Tactics*

## The Chessboard of Defense

Imagine this scenario: the opposition is charging, probing for a weakness in your defense. Yet, as they approach, they find no gaps—just a perfectly organized wall of defenders, shifting together like pieces on a chessboard. Think of Italy's legendary defensive performance against Spain in the 2012 UEFA European Championship semifinals. Despite relentless Spanish pressure, the Italian backline moved as one cohesive unit, cutting off passing lanes and frustrating the opposition. Every move was calculated, every position deliberate, leaving Spain's attackers with no way through.

Defensive positioning isn't just about standing in the right spot; it's the secret weapon that turns defenders into tacticians and keeps attackers at bay. Let's unlock the science and strategy behind elite positioning and tactics.

## Introduction: The Science of Defensive Positioning

If defending is an art, then positioning is the canvas on which it's drawn. While the mental aspects of defense provide a crucial foundation, a defender's positioning determines whether they succeed or fail in preventing goals. Positioning is about more than just standing in the right place; it involves reading the game, adjusting to the movement of the opposition, and anticipating the next phase of play.

As Christopher Duncan insightfully teaches, "Success is about being in the right place, at the right time, with the right mindset." His philosophy doesn't just apply to life but also to success in defensive soccer. In this chapter, we'll explore the nuances of both zonal and man-marking systems, breaking down their strengths, challenges, and how to apply them effectively. Let's dig into the positioning techniques and tactics that can elevate your defensive game.

# Visual Aid 1: Defensive Positioning in Different Game Phases

## A. Back Four Defending Deep

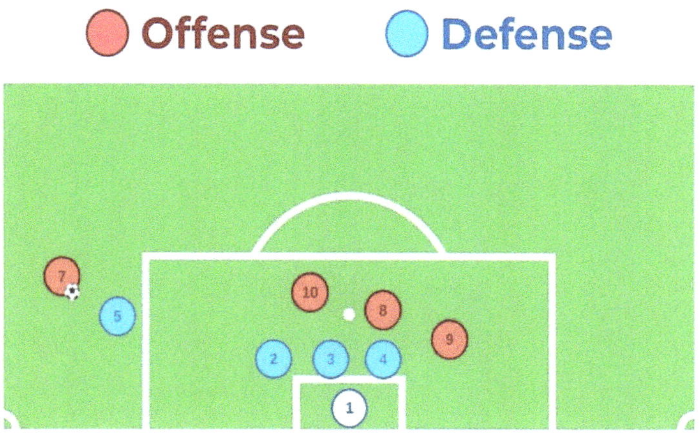


## B. Back Four Covering Space in the Midfield

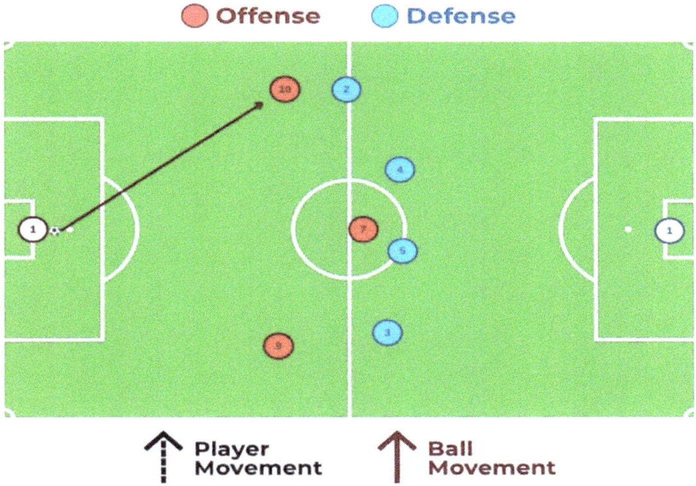

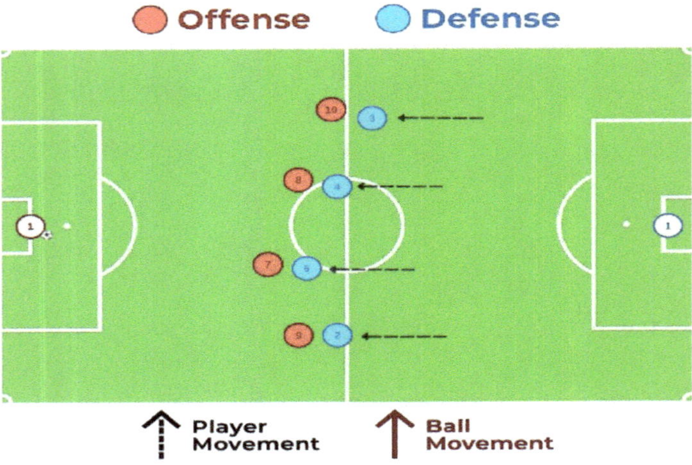



In this chapter, we will break down the critical aspects of defensive positioning, focusing on both individual and team tactics. You'll learn how to place yourself optimally in various game situations, read the opposition's strategies, and work cohesively with teammates to create a nearly impenetrable defensive unit.

## The Importance of Defensive Structure

At the heart of any great defense is a well-established structure. Think of it as building a house— you need a solid foundation. The best defenders control space by positioning themselves effectively and understanding angles. As Christopher Michael Duncan puts it, "Your success in any field comes from the structure you build around yourself."

This principle is central to defensive soccer, where a solid structure often leads to a resilient defense.

# Visual Aid 2: The Art of Defensive Structure and Zonal Defense

In the following defensive scenarios, the objective is to force the ball to the outside and not allow the attacking team to penetrate through the middle.

### A. Defense in Compact Shape Centrally Controlling Passing Lanes

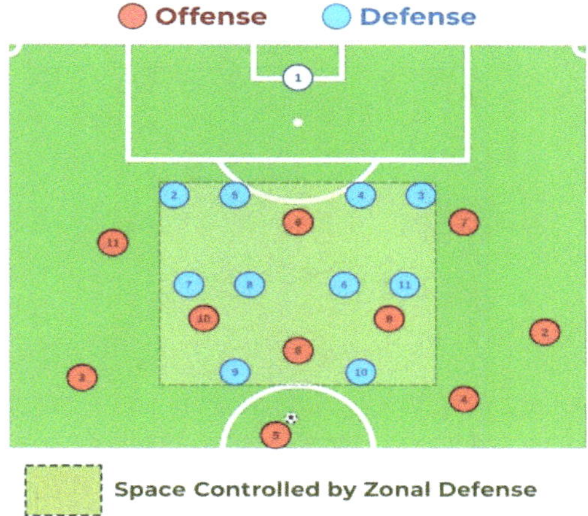


### B. Defense Shifting Compactly, Collectively, and Timely when the Ball Moves

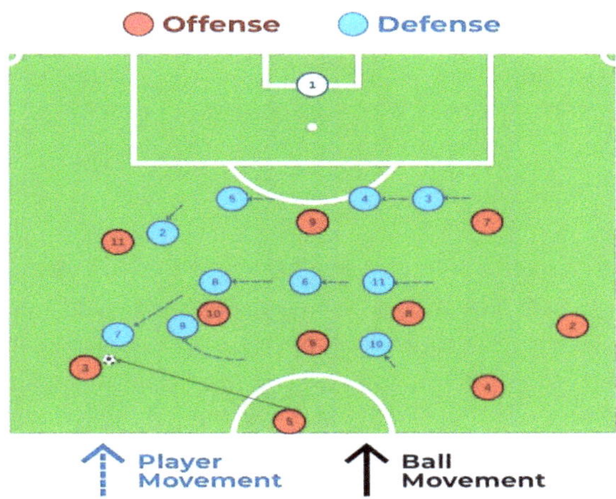

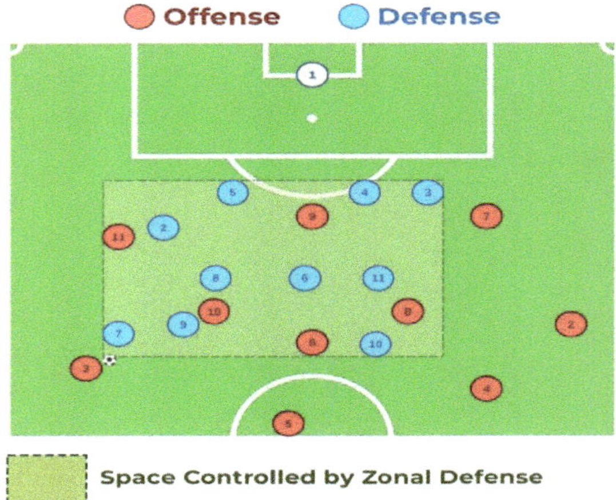



These visuals demonstrate the synergy between compactness and zonal control, helping defenders understand how elite defenders balance controlling space and maintaining defensive shape, eliminating or reducing passing lanes.

**Controlling Space: The Art of Zonal Defense**

Zonal defending is about controlling space rather than chasing opponents. Properly executed, zonal defense limits attacking options, making it difficult for the opposing team to penetrate. Arrigo Sacchi, the Italian coach who revolutionized defensive tactics in the 1980s, once said: "The defenders' primary concern isn't marking an opponent but reducing the space in which the opponent can operate." This approach captures the essence of zonal defending.

Unlike man-marking, where defenders stick tightly to specific players, zonal defense prioritizes structure and collective movement to guard key areas of the pitch. While man-marking focuses on neutralizing individual threats, zonal defending excels in maintaining team shape and adaptability. Both systems have unique strengths and challenges, which we'll explore further in the next section.

**Key Principles of Zonal Defense**

### 1.   Awareness of Your Zone

Understanding the boundaries of your zone is fundamental in zonal defense. Your role isn't to chase opponents but to control space, ensuring attackers find no easy path forward. Staying disciplined prevents the defense from becoming stretched or disorganized. For example, when an attacker drifts wide, resist the urge to follow unless they pose an immediate threat—this keeps the defensive line compact and effective.

In the 2010 FIFA World Cup, Spain's defense showcased this principle perfectly during their match against Germany. When Mesut Özil made a dangerous run into the wide areas, instead of chasing him, the Spanish defenders held their positions in the central zones. This discipline blocked passing options into the box and forced Özil to take a less threatening route, ultimately neutralizing the attack.

### 2.   Proactive Positioning

Anticipating the opposition's movements can make the difference between disrupting a play and conceding a chance. Being proactive means adjusting your position based on the ball's trajectory and the attackers' tendencies rather than waiting to react. For instance, if the opposing winger shows signs of cutting inside, subtly shift inward to close the gap before they can exploit it. This readiness creates an advantage, giving defenders control over their zone.

### 3.   Communication: The Glue of a Cohesive Defense

Communication is the thread that ties zonal defense together. Without it, even the best-positioned backline can falter. Clear instructions like "mark left," "cover back," or "step up" help synchronize movements and ensure no gaps are left exposed. Vocal leaders, such as the goalkeeper or center-back, often guide the team, calling out threats and orchestrating shifts.

Communication also extends beyond words. Gestures and eye contact can reinforce alignment, especially in noisy environments. A simple rule: Communicate early, often, and with purpose.

To improve defensive communication during training sessions, teams can incorporate drills that emphasize verbal and nonverbal coordination. For example, defenders can practice using short, consistent codes like "switch" or "hold" during small-sided games to manage transitions. Another effective exercise is running zonal marking simulations where players rely on hand signals or pointing to mark spaces and shift as a unit. These habits, honed in training, transform individual defenders into an impenetrable collective.

### 4.  Movement as a Unit

A synchronized defensive line minimizes gaps and eliminates scoring opportunities. When one defender shifts, the others must follow to maintain compactness. For example, if the ball moves from the left flank to the center, the entire backline should shift collectively to ensure no attacker can exploit the space. Disjointed movement creates vulnerabilities; unity keeps the defense airtight. Teams like AC Milan under Arrigo Sacchi in the late 1980s exemplified this principle perfectly. Their backline moved as one, compressing space horizontally and vertically to deny opponents any room to operate. Similarly, Atletico Madrid under Diego Simeone is renowned for their tight, unified defensive block, shifting seamlessly to nullify threats and force attackers into less dangerous areas.
These examples highlight how disciplined, collective movement can neutralize even the most potent offenses.

### 5.  Layered Defense

Zonal defending thrives on depth, with multiple layers of coverage to stifle attackers. Beyond the backline, midfielders play a crucial role in closing passing lanes and supporting defensive efforts. For instance, while the defenders track attackers within their zones, midfielders apply pressure on the ball carrier, making it difficult for them to find a viable passing option. This multi-tiered approach forces attackers into mistakes and reduces their ability to create meaningful chances.

*Humor:* **A zonal defender joked, "I don't follow players—I just follow the ball. And if the ball follows a player, I might reconsider!"**

**Man-Marking with Purpose: Shutting Down Key Players**

While zonal defending controls space, man-marking focuses on limiting the influence of specific players. Against opponents like Messi or Ronaldo, it's sometimes necessary to track them closely. Bobby Moore, the legendary English defender, once said, "Good defending is about anticipation and positioning, not about putting out fires." This emphasizes that man-marking is about staying one step ahead, ensuring opponents are neutralized before they can pose a threat.

A prime example of this was Ander Herrera's remarkable man-marking job on Eden Hazard during Manchester United's victory over Chelsea in 2017. Herrera shadowed Hazard relentlessly, cutting off passing lanes and denying him time on the ball, effectively neutralizing one of the Premier League's most dangerous attackers. This performance not only showcased the discipline and anticipation required for man-marking but also highlighted its potential to change the course of a game.

**Visual Aid 3: Man-Marking: Denying Key Players Time and Space**

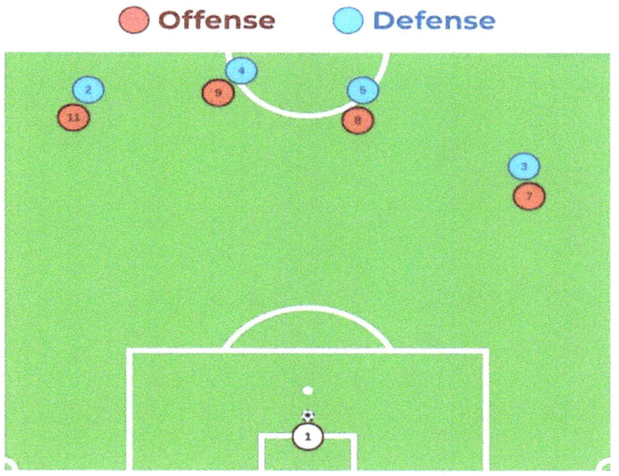

*Humor:* **A defender said, "I didn't mark him out of the game—I just made him consider a career change!"**

## Effective Man-Marking Tactics

— ***Stay Close Without Overcommitting:*** Keep close to your opponent without diving or lounging in too soon.

— ***Anticipate Their Movements:*** Read body language and where they'll go next.

— ***Know Their Tendencies:*** Study opponents' movements to understand if they favor cutting inside or staying central, left or right footed etc.

## Reading the Game: Anticipation over Reaction

To excel in positioning, a defender must learn to anticipate the game's flow. Legends like Maldini, Beckenbauer, Puyol, and van Dijk made their mark by seeing plays unfold before they happened. Anticipation allows a defender to position themselves optimally, preventing danger before it occurs.

## Anticipation vs. Reaction

— ***Anticipation***: Predicts where the ball or player will be based on patterns, body language, and game flow. It allows early positioning to disrupt threats before they materialize.

— ***Reaction***: Occurs after the play has developed, often leaving defenders at a disadvantage.

## Why Anticipation is Superior

— ***Energy Efficiency:*** Anticipation reduces unnecessary movement.

— ***Proactivity:*** It forces attackers to adapt to the defender.

— ***Control:*** Early positioning limits the attacker's options.

***Example:*** A defender who anticipates a winger cutting inside positions themselves inward, intercepting the pass. A reactive defender only adjusts after the pass, often arriving too late.

**Visual Aid 4: How Defenders Anticipate and Read the Game**

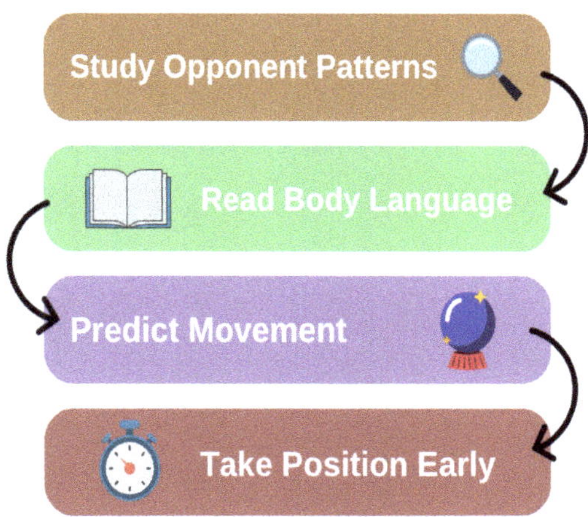



**Offside Basics**

**Scenario: Team A (Attacking) vs. Team B (Defending)**

- **Who Can Be Offside?**

Only players from the attacking team (Team A) can be called offside, and only when they are in the defending team's (Team B's) half of the field.

- **What Does "Offside Position" Mean?**

An attacking player is in an offside position if:

They are closer to the opponent's goal than both the ball and the second-to-last defender.

However, being in an offside position is not a foul unless the player is actively involved in the play (e.g., touching the ball, interfering with an opponent, or gaining an advantage).

**Passing and Offside**

If two attacking players get behind the defensive line:

- The player in possession of the ball (Attacker 1) must pass to a teammate (Attacker 2) who is behind the ball at the time of the pass.

- If Attacker 2 is ahead of the ball when it's passed, they will be called offside.

In summary, to stay onside, the attacking player receiving the ball must either stay behind the second-to-last defender or stay behind the ball when the pass is made.

### Visual Aid 5: Offside Rule Breakdown: "What Counts as Offside?"

A. Attacker #11 is in an offside position. However, there is not an offside violation yet since the ball has not been passed.

**B.** Attacker #11 is now in violation because he is now in possession of the ball past the second-to-last defender.

**C.** In this alternate scenario, Attacker #9 is not in violation because he had possession of the ball before passing the second-to-last defender. However, if he passes to #11, who is in an offside position, #11 would be in violation.

**The Offside Trap: Outsmarting Attackers with Precision**

The offside rule may seem complex, but for defenders, it's a valuable tool. Teams like Arrigo Sacchi's AC Milan famously used the offside trap to catch attackers in offside positions, rendering them ineffective. The key to an offside trap? Timing and coordination.

To master this tactic, teams can practice with a simple yet effective training drill. Set up a defensive line of four players against a group of attackers. A coach or neutral player acts as the playmaker, feeding balls into attacking runs. The defenders must work together to maintain a straight line and step up in unison the moment the pass is played, aiming to catch the attackers offside. To add realism, vary the timing and direction of passes, challenging the defenders to react quickly and in sync.

Drills like this build the awareness and precision needed to execute offside traps successfully, turning them into a potent weapon against even the most skillful opponents.

**The Offside Trap: Timing and Coordination**

The offside trap is as much about timing as it is about coordination. Each defender must step forward simultaneously, keeping attackers offside while staying aware of the referee's position.
Missteps in timing or lack of coordination can leave attackers onside, creating easy goal-scoring chances.

# Visual Aid 6: The Offside Trap in Action

A. The lone striker is in an onside position.

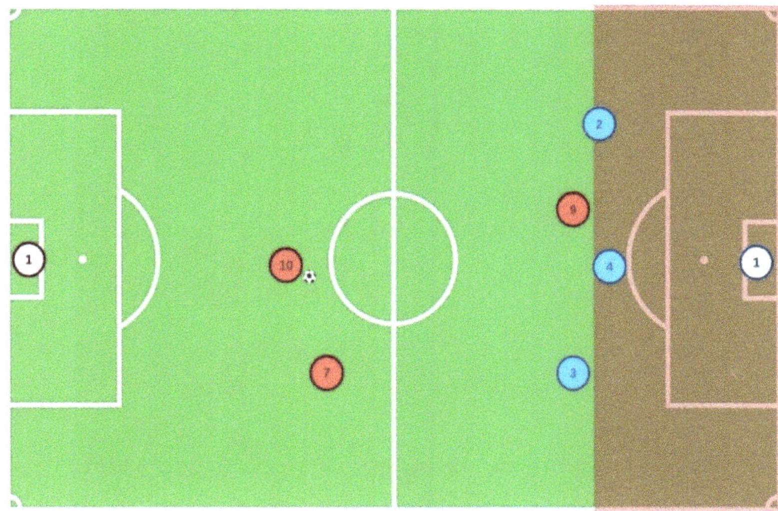

B. The defenders anticipate a pass to the lone striker, and all step forward collectively, coordinately, and timely before the ball is passed, leaving the lone striker in an offside position.

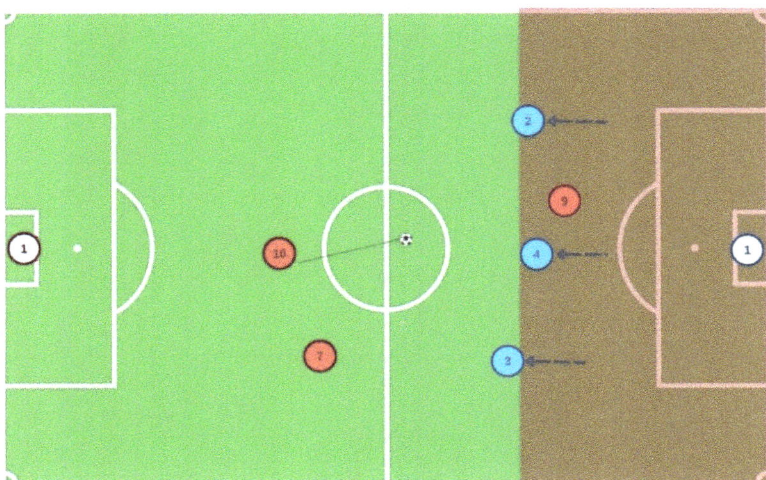

C. **The loan striker receives the ball in an offside position, resulting in an offside.**

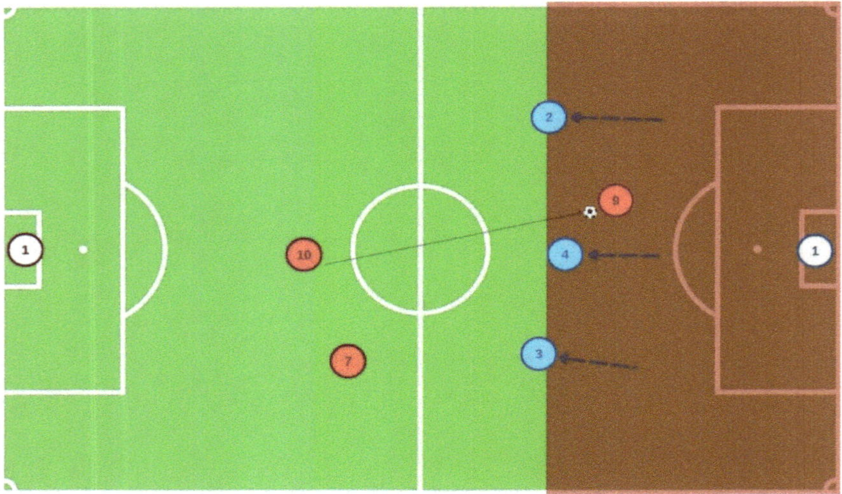

## Conclusion: Laying the Foundations for Tactical Mastery

Mastering defensive positioning and tactics transforms defenders into architects of the game. Whether controlling space with zonal defense, shadowing opponents through man-marking, or executing the offside trap, positioning remains the cornerstone of elite defending.

These strategies empower teams to neutralize threats and dictate the flow of play.

# Visual Aid 7: Key Principles of Defensive Positioning

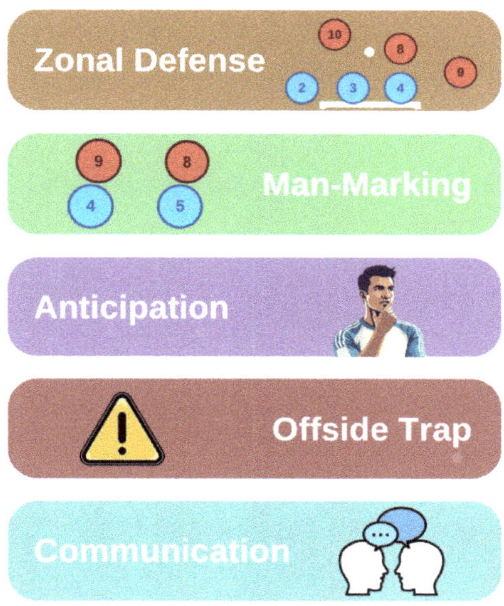


## The Ripple Effect of Strong Defense

Great defensive positioning doesn't just prevent goals—it inspires confidence across the entire team. When defenders consistently make the right choices, it frees up midfielders and forwards to focus on attacking, knowing the backline is secure. Beyond the pitch, mastering these tactics reflects life's broader lessons: being prepared, reading situations, and responding proactively. In soccer, as in life, success often comes down to being in the right place at the right time—and knowing exactly what to do once you're there.

## Memorable Takeaways (with Reflective Prompts)

1. **Master the Art of Zonal Defense**

   — Focus on controlling space rather than solely  marking opponents.

- Always stay disciplined within your zone to prevent gaps in the defense.

- ***Remember***. A compact, cohesive defensive line is your greatest asset.

**Reflective Prompt:**

What steps can you take to improve your awareness of space and your role in a defensive structure?

2. **Man-Marking with Precision**

- Use man-marking selectively to neutralize dangerous players.

- Anticipate your opponent's movements and act proactively, not reactively.

- Stay composed—man-marking is about mental sharpness, not just physical ability.

**Reflective Prompt**

How can you balance focusing on an individual player while maintaining awareness of the overall game?

3. **The Power of Anticipation**

- Read the game like a chess master—plan your moves ahead of time.

- Anticipation reduces your need for last-ditch tackles and energy-draining recovery runs.

**Reflective Prompt**

In what ways can studying the body language of attackers help you predict their next move?

4. **Master the Offside Trap**

— Timing and coordination are everything—practice stepping up as a defensive unit.

— Communicate constantly to ensure everyone is aligned and aware of their role.

**Reflective Prompt**

Can you recall a time when your team successfully executed an offside trap? What made it work?

1. **Teamwork and Communication are Non-Negotiable**

— Every great defensive unit relies on clear communication and trust.

— Give and receive instructions openly to ensure your backline moves as one.

**Reflective Prompt**

How can you improve communication with your teammates during high pressure moments?

**Summary and Bread Crumbs for Future Chapters**

This chapter provided a deep dive into defensive positioning and tactics, covering zonal systems, man-marking, and the offside trap. These concepts are foundational to becoming a smarter, more effective defender. As you continue to refine your skills, consider revisiting the visuals and prompts in this chapter during your training sessions. Use them to practice defensive positioning, communication, and timing in real-time scenarios.

In the next chapter, we'll dive into tackling and interceptions, exploring how defenders physically win the ball. Get ready to learn the art of clean tackles, effective positioning for interceptions, and executing these maneuvers with precision and timing.

# CHAPTER 3: Tackling and Interceptions —The Art of Winning the Ball

**Where Defense Meets Artistry**

Consider this image of a forward charging toward your goal, eyes locked on glory. The crowd holds its breath. Then, with surgical precision, a defender lunges, winning the ball cleanly. The forward looks stunned. This isn't just football—it's artistry in motion.

Tackling and interceptions are more than defensive maneuvers; they are moments of brilliance that inspire teammates, disrupt opponents, and often change the tide of a game. Think of Fabio Cannavaro's iconic interception during the 2006 FIFA World Cup quarter-final against Germany. As the clock ticked down, Cannavaro anticipated a critical pass, surged forward, and not only won possession but set up the counterattack that led to Italy's decisive goal. Plays like this remind us how a well-executed defensive move can define the outcome of an entire match. Let's delve into these pivotal skills that transform defenders into game-changers.

**Introduction: The Skills that Define Defensive Mastery**

Defending is an art of reclamation—taking back control and dictating the flow of the game. Tackling and interceptions are not just about breaking up plays; they are about imposing your will on the pitch. These skills represent the essence of defensive mastery, combining physical prowess with mental acuity. Tackling symbolizes direct confrontation, while interceptions highlight anticipation and patience.

How these skills are learned and applied often depends on the defensive style employed. In a high-press system, tackling becomes an aggressive tool to win the ball back higher up the pitch, disrupting the opponent's rhythm and forcing mistakes. In contrast, deep-block defending relies more heavily on well-timed interceptions, where patience and positioning are paramount to stifling attacking threats.

By mastering these techniques, defenders adapt to different tactical demands, making them indispensable to any team's strategy.

## Part 1: Tackling—The Power of the Perfect Challenge

### The Precision of Tackling: More than Just a Physical Skill

A tackle isn't just a physical act—it's a statement. Success depends on discipline, timing, and technique. As Rio Ferdinand aptly noted, "Anyone can make a tackle, but timing is everything. The right tackle can change a game." This perspective underscores the transformative potential of a well-executed tackle.

To refine timing and technique, defenders can practice a drill known as the Shadow Tackle Drill. In this exercise, two players (1 V 1) face off in a confined space, such as a 10x10-yard grid. The attacking player dribbles while the defender shadows closely, waiting for the perfect moment to execute a tackle.
The goal is to improve anticipation and timing while minimizing unnecessary physical contact.
By repeatedly engaging in this drill, players can sharpen their instincts and build confidence in real-game scenarios.

### Timing: The Key to an Effective Tackle

Tackling isn't about lunging in; it's about waiting for the perfect moment. As John Terry said, "A last-ditch tackle is an art. It's about judging distance, speed, and most of all, guts." A defender's ability to wait, observe, and then strike defines their effectiveness.
Think of tackling as chess, where the best players calculate several moves ahead.

### Real-Life Humor

During a youth game, a determined defender, laser-focused on stopping an attacker, boldly shouted, "Not today!" as he lunged forward—only to miss the ball entirely and land flat on his stomach. Without missing a beat, his teammate remarked with a grin, "Looks like it's not today for you either!" Moments like these remind us that even in the heat of competition, soccer has a way of keeping us humble and lighthearted.

To reiterate John Terry's point further, "a last-ditch tackle is an art."

**Types of Tackling Techniques: Front, Slide, Block Tackles, and Toe Poke**

**Each tackle technique serves a unique purpose:**

- **Front Tackle:** A direct, head-on challenge.

- **Slide Tackle:** Riskier but effective in desperate situations.

- **Block Tackle:** Focused on absorbing impact while reclaiming possession.

- **Toe Poke Tackle:** A subtle maneuver to nudge the ball away in tight situations.

**Visual Aid 1: Types of Tackling Techniques**

**Front Tackle**

**Slide Tackle**

**Block Tackle**

**Toe Poke Tackle**

**Motivational Element:** *A tackle isn't just about dispossessing an opponent—it's about inspiring confidence in your team and asserting dominance over the opposition.*

**Real-Life Humor:** *"There's a running joke among defenders: If you finish a game with clean shorts, you didn't work hard enough." Grass stains and scuffed knees might as well be badges of honor.*

**Part 2: Interceptions—Mastering Anticipation and Control**

**The Art of Anticipation: Reading the Game**

Intercepting is about seeing the play before it unfolds. Italian legend Paolo Maldini famously remarked, "If I have to make a tackle, then I have already made a mistake." Interceptions epitomize defensive intelligence, requiring defenders to interpret body language, predict passes, and disrupt play without a tackle.

# Visual Aid 2: The Art of Anticipation

*This illustration shows how a defender (blue uniform) anticipates a passing lane and cuts off a pass to the attacker (red uniform)*

**Timing and Execution: The Heart of an Interception**

Interceptions are the quieter sibling of tackles. They may not draw cheers, but their impact is undeniable. A perfectly timed interception can dismantle an attack before it begins, as demonstrated by Fabio Cannavaro during Italy's 2006 World Cup run.
Cannavaro's instinctive interceptions against Germany showcased the power of defensive foresight.

To enhance interception skills, players can use the Pass Interception Drill. In this exercise, (2 V 1) three players form a triangle. Two players pass the ball back and forth, while the third positions themselves in the middle, anticipating and attempting to intercept the pass. The focus is on reading body language, recognizing passing angles, and timing the interception to perfection. Repetition of this drill not only sharpens instincts but also builds the confidence to disrupt plays in competitive matches.

**Storytelling Element:**

Each successful interception is a psychological victory, leaving attackers second-guessing their choices and creating opportunities
for counterattacks.

**When Not to Tackle: Bravery, Restraint, and Discipline**

Sometimes, the best decision is to stay on your feet.
Jockeying an opponent—guiding them into less dangerous areas—is a vital defensive skill.
Patience here demonstrates bravery and composure.

# Visual Aid 3: The Jockeying Technique

**Humor:** *In a youth match, a defender jockeyed an attacker so persistently that the frustrated forward eventually dribbled the ball out of bounds. The defender joked afterward,*
*"Patience wins every time!"*

## Conclusion: The Transformative Power of Tackling and Interceptions

Tackling and intercepting aren't just defensive maneuvers—they're moments that shift the momentum of a match. A well-timed tackle can ignite a team's energy, while a precise interception stifles the opponent's rhythm. Mastering these skills elevates defenders from reactive players to proactive architects of the game. They embody the essence of defensive brilliance, leaving attackers unsettled and teammates inspired.

### Lessons beyond the Game

The discipline, anticipation, and restraint required for tackling and intercepting mirror the values needed to navigate life's challenges. A tackle teaches us to seize opportunities boldly, while an interception reflects the importance of foresight and preparation.

Together, they remind us that defense isn't just about holding the line—it's about creating new possibilities. Whether on the pitch or off, these skills teach us to think ahead, act decisively, and inspire those around us.

### Memorable Takeaways (with Reflective Prompts)

- **Precision Tackling:** Masterful tackling requires timing, technique, and discipline.

**Reflective Prompt:** Recall a game where a single tackle changed the outcome. What made it so impactfull?

- **Psychological Edge:** Both skills create mental pressure on opponents.

*Reflective Prompt:* Think of a defensive play that visibly frustrated an opponent. What was its ripple effect?

- **Interception Mastery:** Anticipation can turn defense into attack.

*Reflective Prompt*: **Have you seen a moment where an interception directly led to a goal? Reflect on its significance.**

- **Courage and Restraint:** Defensive bravery is often about standing firm.

*Reflective Prompt*: Consider a time when patience proved to be the bravest choice. How did it change the game?

**Summary and Bread Crumbs for Future Chapters**

Tackling and intercepting are at the heart of defensive dominance. These skills allow defenders to halt attacks, unsettle opponents, and initiate their team's transition into offense.

Chapter 4 will delve into working with goalkeepers and building defensive chemistry—key aspects of creating an unbreakable defensive line and mastering team cohesion.

NOTES

# CHAPTER *4: Working with the Goalkeeper and Defensive Chemistry*

**"The Backbone of Defense"**

Create this picture in your mind: a nail-biting match, your goalkeeper shouts directions as the opposition charges down the field. In this moment, trust, chemistry, and communication are the glue holding the defensive line together. Without them, chaos ensues.
With them, you're an unbreakable fortress.

Take Italy's defensive masterclass in the 2006 World Cup final as an example. With Gianluigi Buffon orchestrating from goal, the defensive line—anchored by Fabio Cannavaro—operated as a seamless unit. Every shout, every gesture, and every step worked in unison to frustrate a relentless French attack. Cannavaro's ability to read the game, paired with Buffon's vocal leadership, ensured Italy's defense remained resolute, ultimately paving the way for their triumph in the penalty shootout.

This chapter delves into the art of defensive unity: the relationship between defenders and goalkeepers, the nuances of defensive chemistry, and the mental toughness required to build an impenetrable line. Let's uncover how this synergy forms the backbone of an unstoppable defense.

**Introduction: The Collective Effort of Defense**

Defending in soccer is not a solo act—it's a carefully choreographed performance that depends on trust, communication, and chemistry among teammates. At the heart of this effort is the goalkeeper, the anchor of the defense, guiding the backline to form an impenetrable unit.

Consider iconic partnerships like Virgil van Dijk and Alisson Becker at Liverpool, where seamless communication and mutual understanding transformed their team into a defensive powerhouse.

Their collaboration exemplifies how trust and chemistry can elevate defensive performance to an elite level.

In this chapter, we explore the partnership between goalkeepers and defenders, the importance of defensive chemistry, and the principles that create a strong, cohesive defensive unit.

You'll discover actionable insights, from communication drills to strategies for building trust, celebrating the art of defensive collaboration—whether you're a rising star or a seasoned veteran.

### The Goalkeeper-Defender Relationship: A Silent Conversation

### A Leader behind the Scenes

The goalkeeper is not only a last line of defense but also the organizer of the defensive structure.

Through clear and decisive communication—often conveyed in just a few gestures or words—they guide their defenders to anticipate threats and respond in unison.

### Key Aspects of the Goalkeeper-Defender Partnership

- **Trust and Communication:** Goalkeepers have a panoramic view of the field, making their instructions crucial for defensive positioning and marking. Whether they're calling to hold the line, drop deep, or press forward, defenders must trust and respond to these commands to maintain a cohesive and effective defense.

- **Decision Making:** In high-pressure moments, the ability of both the goalkeeper and defenders to make fast, confident decisions is paramount. Whether choosing to tackle or hold, press or delay, each split-second decision affects the next, creating a ripple effect across the entire backline. A solid partnership requires a mutual understanding of when each player will take charge to avoid hesitation or over-committing.

- **Practical Exercise:** Reactive Defensive Drill: Set up a game scenario where defenders and the goalkeeper must react to various attacking cues. Position attackers to simulate different situations—such as through balls, wide crosses, and direct runs.
The goalkeeper calls out commands like "Step up!" or "Hold!"

while defenders adjust their positioning and actions accordingly. This exercise builds decision-making confidence and reinforces the importance of clear communication under pressure, ensuring defenders instinctively know when to tackle, delay, or cover based on the goalkeeper's cues.

- **Commanding the Box:** A strong goalkeeper not only stops shots but also controls the penalty area. Defenders need to know when their keeper will step out to claim crosses or sweep behind the backline. Clear communication on who commands each play is critical; any miscommunication in these situations can lead to costly errors.

- **Distribution and Play-Building:** Modern goalkeepers, like Manchester City's Ederson, are often the first playmakers. Their distribution can ignite a counterattack or set up possession play from the back.
  Defenders play a crucial role in this by reading and supporting the goalkeeper's passes, working together to transition from defense to attack smoothly.

- **Resilience:** In moments of intense pressure, both goalkeepers and defenders must show resilience, maintaining focus and composure even when the odds seem stacked against them. Resilience means recovering quickly from setbacks, such as a conceded goal or a defensive mistake, and remaining mentally tough and unwavering throughout the game.

Consider Liverpool's legendary resilience in the 2005 Champions League final. Trailing 3–0 at halftime against AC Milan, their defense and goalkeeper Jerzy Dudek faced relentless pressure as they clawed their way back into the game. After leveling the score, Dudek's incredible double save in extra time and his heroics in the penalty shootout became iconic examples of mental toughness and composure. This display of resilience transformed what seemed like an inevitable defeat into one of the greatest comebacks in football history.

This mental endurance is vital in challenging matches, allowing the defense to reset and stand firm in the face of adversity, knowing that even in the direst situations, persistence can lead to triumph.

***Real-Life Humor:* During a recreational league match, a center-back yelled, "Mark someone! Anyone!" only to hear the goalkeeper quip, "You first!" Despite the chuckles that followed, the team quickly regained focus, tightened their marking, and successfully cleared the next corner kick—showing how humor and quick adjustments go hand in hand in building defensive chemistry.**

**Motivational Take: For Younger Players**

A goalkeeper's voice is your guide; their confidence fuels your actions. Imagine your goalkeeper as the lighthouse guiding your ship to safety—always listening, always trusting.

*Reflection Prompt:* Think about your last game or training session. How often did you communicate with your goalkeeper? Were their instructions clear, and did you respond confidently? Set a goal for your next match to actively listen for their cues and ensure your movements align with their guidance.

## Visual Aid 1: How Goalkeepers Organize Defensive Setups

## Defensive Chemistry: Building a Unit, Not Just a Line

Defensive chemistry is about moving as one. Great defenses don't operate in isolation; each player knows the roles and positioning of others. Like a well-practiced dance, defensive coordination keeps the line intact and strong.

Take Giorgio Chiellini and Leonardo Bonucci, the backbone of Italy's defense for over a decade. Their partnership, highlighted during Italy's Euro 2020 triumph, was a masterclass in defensive chemistry. Chiellini's physicality and tactical awareness perfectly complemented Bonucci's composure and ball-playing ability. Their understanding of each other's strengths and tendencies allowed them to anticipate movements, close down gaps, and support one another seamlessly.

This kind of synergy is the foundation of a successful defensive unit, proving that trust and coordination transform a line of individuals into an unbreakable wall.

Chemistry relies on understanding how teammates instinctively play, react, and adapt under different scenarios. Noticing and internalizing each player's tendencies—whether it's their preferred foot, typical movements, or how they handle pressure—helps predict and respond more effectively during play. When teammates grasp these nuances, they start anticipating each other's actions, leading to smoother, more synchronized gameplay. This level of chemistry often sets successful teams apart, as it transforms individual skills into a cohesive, dynamic unit.

From a defender's perspective, studying an opponent's tendencies is a crucial strategy for gaining the upper hand in duels. By analyzing an attacker's habits—like how they approach one-on-one situations, their go-to moves, or which direction they tend to favor—a defender can anticipate the attacker's next move and counter it more effectively.

Consider Virgil van Dijk's exceptional reading of the game. In a 2019 Premier League match against Tottenham, Van Dijk faced a two-on-one situation against Moussa Sissoko and Son Heung-min.

Knowing Sissoko was less confident shooting with his left foot, Van Dijk subtly steered him away from his stronger side, forcing a rushed, off-target shot.

This moment highlighted Van Dijk's ability to read his opponent's tendencies, effectively neutralizing a dangerous counterattack.

This deep understanding helps defenders disrupt an opponent's rhythm, forcing them into less comfortable positions and increasing the chance of making successful tackles or interceptions.

*Quote for Inspiration:* **"Defending is an art. You have to anticipate and paint the picture before the attacker does." – Maldini**

**Motivational Take: For All Players**

Chemistry builds trust, and trust creates unity.
When defenders anticipate and adapt to each other, they evolve into an unbreakable force.

## Visual Aid 2: Coordinated Defensive Line Movement Positioned Centrally in Relation to the Ball

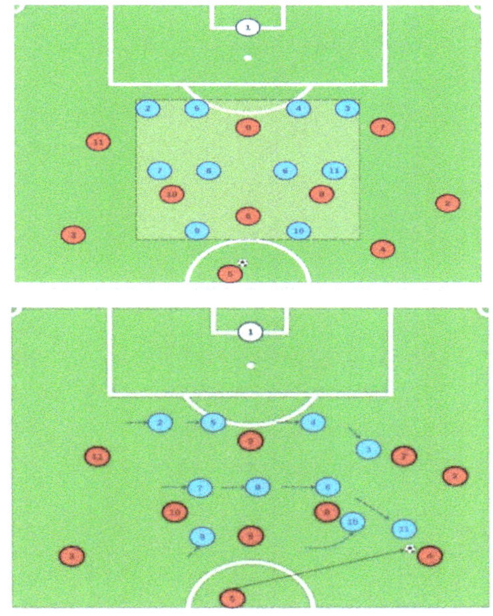

## The Principles of Defense: Pressure, Cover, Balance, and Compactness

These four elements form the backbone of effective defensive strategy and is the foundation of any cohesive defense. Together, they create a coordinated and impenetrable system that anticipates and neutralizes threats. Let's dive deeper into each principle:

### Pressure: The First Line of Resistance

Pressure begins with the defender closest to the ball. This defender's role is to challenge the attacker immediately, aiming to disrupt their rhythm, delay the play, or force an error. Pressure isn't always about winning the ball instantly—it's about creating discomfort and dictating where the play goes.

### Key Goals of Pressure

- Slow the attacker down and allow teammates to regroup.

- Force the attacker into predictable movements, such as turning backward or to their weaker foot.

- Influence where the ball is played, ideally toward less dangerous areas of the field.

Example: Think of a midfielder charging at an attacker with the ball, pushing them toward the sideline. By closing down space and limiting options, the defender gives their teammates time to reorganize and prepare for the next phase of play.

### Cover: The Safety Net

The second defender provides cover for the one applying pressure. Positioned a few steps behind and at an angle, this defender is ready to step in if the first defender is bypassed. Cover ensures that no single mistake leads to an immediate scoring opportunity.

**Key Goals of Cover**

- Provide immediate support to the pressuring defender.

- Anticipate and intercept passes or deflections.

- Maintain defensive depth and prevent attackers from penetrating central areas.

*Example*: Picture a center-back stepping up to confront an attacker while their defensive partner stays slightly behind and to the side, ready to intercept any through ball or block a run.

### A.  Balance: Maintaining Defensive Integrity

Balance involves the defenders who are not directly pressuring or covering. Their role is to ensure the team's shape isn't compromised, especially on the weak side (the side of the field opposite the ball). Balanced defenders monitor potential threats, such as unmarked attackers or quick switches of play, while keeping the defensive line organized.

**Key Goals of Balance**

- Prevent attackers from exploiting gaps left by pressing defenders.

- Maintain a cohesive defensive line, avoiding overcommitting to one side.

- Be prepared to handle long passes or counterattacks.

*Example:* If the ball is on the right wing, the left-back and opposite center-back remain alert to potential cross-field passes or runs into space, ensuring that the team isn't caught off guard.

### B.  Compactness: Shrinking the Field for the Opposition

Compactness refers to the defensive unit working together to reduce the amount of usable space for the opposing team. By closing gaps between defenders and midfielders, compactness forces attackers into narrow, less threatening areas. This principle is particularly crucial when defending deep in your own half.

**Key Goals of Compactness:**

- Minimize the spaces attackers can exploit, especially between the lines.

- Funnel play toward the wings, where it's harder to score from.

- Maintain a disciplined shape that adjusts quickly as the ball moves.

*Example:* During a counterattack, the defense quickly retreats into a tight formation, leaving no gaps for attackers to exploit centrally. The opposition is forced wide, where crossing into a crowded penalty area becomes their only option.

## Visual Aid 3: Compact Defense: Shrinking Space for the Opposition

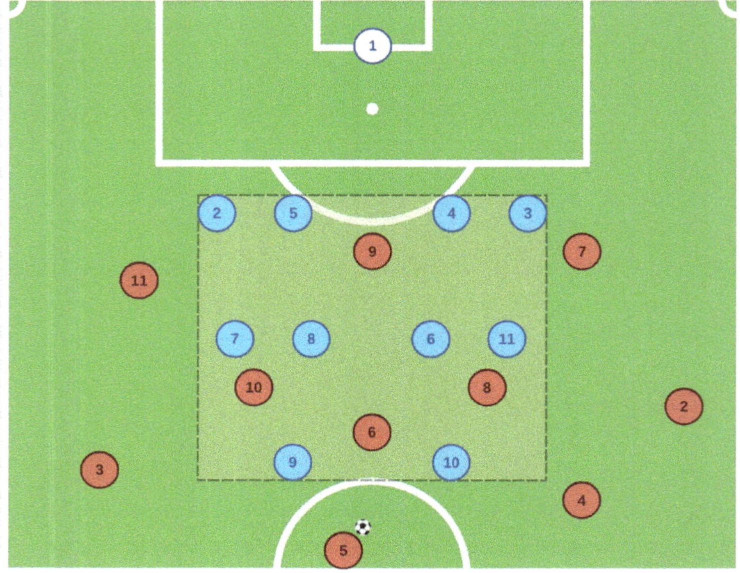

## Compactness: Shrinking the Field for the Opposition

Compactness is the glue that binds pressure, cover, and balance into a cohesive strategy. A compact defensive shape requires players to stay disciplined in their positioning, maintaining close proximity to teammates while adapting fluidly to the movement of the ball.

## Practical Applications of Compactness

a. **Vertical Compactness:** The defensive line and midfield stay close together, reducing the vertical space attackers have to operate. This makes it harder for the opposition to play penetrating passes or take long-range shots.

b. **Horizontal Compactness:** The defense narrows the field by shifting toward the side where the ball is, cutting off passing lanes and reducing opportunities for attackers to switch play effectively.

## Key Benefits:

- It limits the effectiveness of creative attackers who thrive in open spaces.

- It simplifies decision-making by reducing the number of dangerous areas the defense must monitor.

- It creates a psychological barrier for attackers, who feel "crowded out" and forced into low-percentage plays.

*Example:* In a match where a team is leading 1-0, the defense sits deep and compact, denying central spaces while encouraging the opposition to cross from wide areas. The defenders then focus on winning aerial duels or second balls to neutralize the threat.

**Motivational Take: For Defenders of All Levels**

By mastering the principles of defense, you build a foundation for your team's success. Each role, whether pressuring, covering, or balancing, contributes to a cohesive whole.

*Real-Life Humor: After a hard-fought 1-0 victory, Jose Mourinho famously joked, "Our defense was so compact, even water couldn't seep through!" This light-hearted remark encapsulates the essence of defensive unity—when defenders work seamlessly together, they can stifle even the most talented attackers.*

The humor serves as a reminder that a well-organized defense is not just effective but also a source of pride and inspiration for the entire team.

**The 3 R's of Soccer: Reposition, Recuperation, and Redistribution**

After possession is lost, the team quickly moves into action to regain control:

- **Reposition:** Recover shape to defend the opponent's immediate attack.

- **Recuperation:** Work to regain possession as soon as possible.

- **Redistribution:** Once regained, set up an attack or relieve pressure.

**The 3 P's of Soccer: Pressure, Position, and Possession**

These three principles help every defensive unit work efficiently. Let's look at each and see how defenders apply them:

- **Pressure:** The closest defender applies pressure, aiming not to win the ball immediately but to slow the attack and force mistakes.

- **Position:** The second defender positions themselves to back up the first in case they're bypassed, providing a safety net.

- Possession: The third defender, while staying balanced, focuses on regaining control and setting up a counter.

# Visual Aid 4: Roles of First, Second, and Third Defenders

## Motivational Take: For All Defenders

Defending may not be flashy, but every small pressure, position, or regaining possession fuels your team's offense. Think of it as building the play, setting the stage for your team to shine.

## Lessons in Unity and Resilience

The dynamics between defenders and goalkeepers go beyond the pitch, reflecting life's broader themes of trust, communication, coordination, and adaptability. Just as a defensive line functions through shared responsibility and mutual understanding, success in any endeavor requires individuals to harmonize their efforts for a greater purpose.

Building defensive chemistry teaches us the value of knowing our strengths, recognizing the tendencies of those around us, and adapting seamlessly to shifting circumstances. The resilience demanded in moments of pressure—recovering after setbacks and staying composed in adversity—mirrors the mental toughness needed to navigate challenges off the field.

Ultimately, the principles of defense remind us that strength lies in unity. Whether in soccer or life, collaboration, trust, and clear communication transform groups into cohesive teams capable of overcoming the toughest opponents.

**Conclusion: Building the Fortress**

The principles of communication, trust, and defensive chemistry all work together to build a strong defensive unit. Remember, great defenses rely on teamwork over individual brilliance. Applying pressure, cover, balance, and compactness consistently strengthen your team's ability to fend off attacks.

In the next chapter, we'll explore Defending Set Pieces: Mastering High-Pressure Moments—crucial situations where defensive discipline and unity can mean the difference between victory and defeat.

**Memorable Takeaways (with Reflective Prompts):**

- ***Trust your Goalkeeper:*** A goalkeeper is the commander of the defense. Trust their calls and work as a cohesive unit to secure a strong line of defense.

***Reflective Prompt:*** Think of a recent game where a single call made a significant impact on the play. How did you respond, and what might you do differently next time?

- ***Pressure, Cover, Balance:*** Master these essential defensive principles. Know your role as the first, second, or third defender.

***Reflective Prompt:*** Reflect on a play where you were one of these defenders. How did your positioning affect the overall defensive shape?

- **Compactness is Key:** Tighten the defensive line to reduce space for the opposition, steering them into less favorable areas.

*Reflective Prompt:* When have you successfully closed space to prevent an attack? How might this positioning strengthen your defensive impact?

- ***The 3 P's and 3 R's:*** Understand how pressure, position, possession, reposition, recuperation, and redistribution impact the flow of defensive play.

*Reflective Prompt:* How often do you focus on these principles during a game? Which one needs the most attention for you?

- ***Communication Builds Chemistry:*** Constant communication within the defense ensures proper adjustments, clarity of roles, and strong connections among teammates.

*Reflective Prompt:* Think of a time when communication helped or hindered your defense. What strategies could improve clarity and cohesion?

- **Resilience in the Face of Pressure:** Adversity tests defenders and goalkeepers alike. Recover from setbacks, stay mentally strong, and keep a level head even after a mistake.

*Reflective Prompt:* Recall a moment where resilience made a difference in your game.

How can this experience guide you in future high-stakes scenarios?

## Summary and Bread Crumbs for Future Chapters

We've explored the foundational elements of working as a cohesive defensive unit. The goalkeeper and defenders must stay in harmony, communicating constantly, and applying these principles to minimize the opponent's chances.

In Chapter 5, we'll tackle Defending Set Pieces: Mastering High-Pressure Moments, where precise positioning and timing become critical for defensive success.

# CHAPTER 5: Defending Set Pieces —Mastering High-Pressure Moments

**The Drama of Set Pieces**

It's the 90th minute of a tight match. The opposition prepares for a corner kick that could level the game. The ball swings into the penalty area as players jostle, leap, and scramble. The difference between heartbreak and triumph lies in one moment—your ability to organize, communicate, and execute.

Set pieces are where legends are made and matches are decided. Every defensive move is a high-stakes battle, where preparation meets opportunity under intense pressure. To succeed, defenders must rely on more than instinct—they must implement structured defensive strategies honed through practice. This chapter explores the key elements that turn chaotic moments into opportunities for defensive mastery.

**Introduction: The Moment of Truth**

Set pieces in soccer are much more than tactical drills—they are moments of high drama that demand composure, preparation, and mental toughness. As a defender, your role during these moments often determines the game's outcome.

This chapter is your guide to mastering the art and science of defending set pieces, from organizing defensive walls to winning aerial duels. You'll learn how to turn chaos into control, not just surviving but excelling in soccer's most nerve-wracking situations. Success in these moments stems from preparation—the drills, strategies, and repetitions that ensure composure and precision under pressure. By connecting defensive practice to on-field execution, this chapter equips you to handle any set-piece scenario with confidence and skill.

## Defending Corners: Aerial Duels, Organization, and Marking Systems

Corners are among the most dangerous set pieces, with attackers constantly looking to exploit the slightest defensive lapse. The defender's role is to neutralize this threat with effective organization, strong aerial presence, and sharp communication.

### Zonal, Man-Marking, and Hybrid Systems

**Three strategies dominate corner defense:**

- **Zonal Marking:** Defenders cover specific areas of the penalty box, focusing on the ball. This method prevents dominant attackers from easily exploiting spaces but demands intense focus to close gaps. For example, Italy's 2006 World Cup team excelled in zonal marking, consistently neutralizing set-piece threats through disciplined area coverage.

- **Man-Marking:** Here, defenders tightly track attackers, aiming to prevent them from getting free for headers or shots. However, one mistake by a marker can expose the defense.
  Manchester United often employed man-marking during Nemanja Vidić's era, with the center-backs physically dominating key opponents in crucial moments.

- **Hybrid Marking System:** Combining both strategies, this system balances area control and targeted marking of key players. Liverpool under Jürgen Klopp frequently uses a hybrid approach, blending zonal structures with specific focus on aerial threats like Erling Haaland.

# Visual Aid 1: Corner Marking Systems

## 1.  Zonal Marking

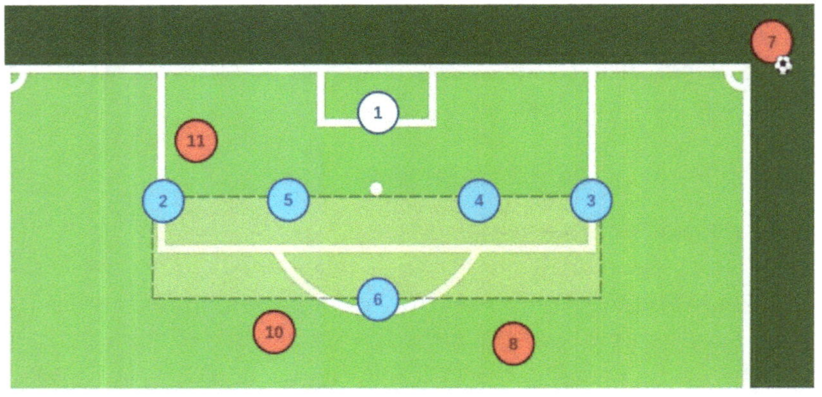

Space Controlled by Zonal Defense

## 2.  Man-Marking

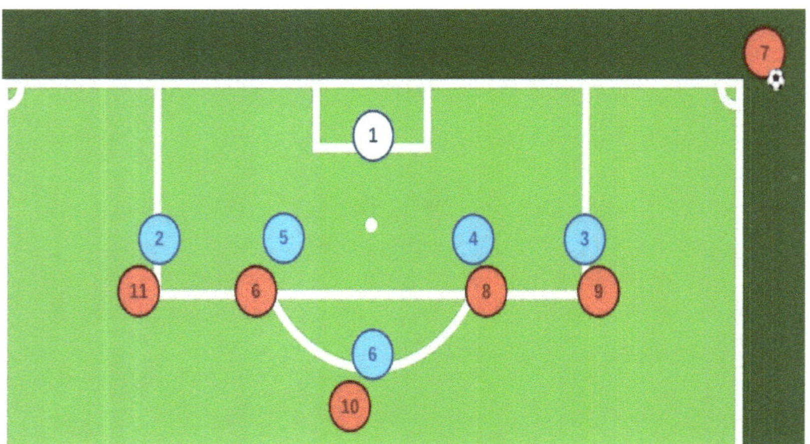

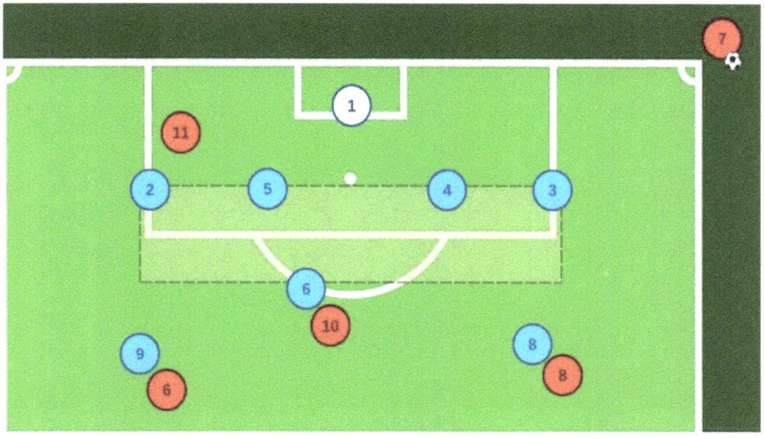

**Space Controlled by Zonal Defense**

## Real-Life Example

Chelsea's hybrid defensive setup in the 2012 Champions League final was pivotal in neutralizing Bayern Munich's corners. Didier Drogba's critical clearance from his zonal position exemplified the value of disciplined execution under pressure.

## Winning the Aerial Duel: Mastering the Air

Aerial battles are where defensive heroes emerge, especially during set pieces. These moments demand precision, timing, and unshakable confidence. Success in the air goes beyond physicality—it's a test of mental readiness, technical skill, and the ability to thrive under pressure.

*Picture this:* It's the 89th minute of a knockout-stage match. As the opposition's star striker positions themselves for a back-post header, your preparation and instincts take over. To clear the danger, you'll need to combine split-second decision-making with technical mastery. Here's how to succeed when the stakes are highest:

**Key Techniques for Winning Aerial Duels**

1. *Positioning:* Anticipate the ball's trajectory and position yourself slightly ahead of your opponent to gain leverage. Subtle body movements can block their run while keeping your actions within the rules. Staying between the attacker and the goal is your first line of defense.

*Drill:* Practice positioning by working on one-on-one aerial challenges. A coach or teammate lobs the ball, and your task is to win the duel without committing a foul.

Rotate roles to enhance both offensive and defensive instincts.

2. *Timing Your Jump:* Jumping at the right moment is critical. Watch the ball closely, judging its flight to time your leap perfectly. Drills focusing on peak jumps and reaction time will improve your ability to dominate in the air.

*Drill:* Use a reaction-based heading exercise, where a ball is dropped or thrown at random heights. Focus on timing your leap to meet the ball at its highest point, mimicking game scenarios.

*Example:* Virgil van Dijk's ability to consistently out-jump opponents in the Premier League showcases his mastery of timing and anticipation.

3. *Using Your Body:* Shield the ball effectively by using your body to create space. A well-placed shoulder or hip can disrupt an opponent's balance, making it harder for them to execute their play without committing a foul.

*Drill:* Practice body positioning by simulating aerial duels with a partner. Alternate between offensive and defensive roles to master how to use your body to create or deny space.

4. *Developing Strength:* Strong neck and upper body muscles are essential for accurate and powerful headers. Incorporate targeted

exercises into your training regimen to build the strength needed for clearances and controlled headers.

*Drill:* Perform resistance band neck exercises or weighted ball header drills. Focus on both the power and direction of your headers during practice.

5. **Confidence under Pressure:** Crowded penalty areas and physical contact are part of the game. Stay mentally tough and focused, ignoring distractions. Confidence in your ability to win the ball can often determine success in these chaotic moments.

*Drill:* Set up a crowded box simulation where multiple players contest for a high ball. The exercise should simulate the physicality and unpredictability of game situations, helping build composure under pressure.

*Example:* Giorgio Chiellini's dominance in aerial duels during Italy's EURO 2020 triumph exemplifies resilience and confidence under immense pressure.

## Training for Aerial Success

Winning aerial duels requires consistent practice to refine your skills and build muscle memory. Incorporate the following drills into your training routine:

1. *Jumping and Heading Drills:* Simulate set-piece situations with teammates, focusing on timing and trajectory.

*Coaching Tip:* Emphasize attacking the ball at its highest point. Encourage players to leap with one knee raised for balance and to protect against challenges from opponents.

2. *Reaction Training:* Work on responding quickly to balls launched at different angles and speeds.

*Coaching Tip:* Use unpredictable delivery methods—such as balls thrown, kicked, or rebounded off walls—to replicate game scenarios.

Encourage players to focus on their initial step and reaction time to ensure maximum effectiveness.

3. ***Strength and Conditioning:*** Build your core and leg strength to maximize your vertical leap and overall stability.

***Coaching Tip:*** Incorporate plyometric exercises such as box jumps and depth jumps to enhance explosive power. Combine these with planks and rotational core exercises for better aerial balance and control.

## Mental Preparation for Aerial Battles

Great defenders aren't just physically prepared—they're mentally sharp. Visualization is a powerful tool to prime yourself for success in aerial duels. Picture yourself timing the perfect leap, outmuscling your opponent, and clearing the ball under pressure.

***Real-Life Example***: During the 2014 World Cup final, Germany's Mats Hummels consistently won aerial duels against Argentina, demonstrating exceptional anticipation and body positioning. His composure and physical dominance neutralized the opposition's set-piece threat, showcasing the critical role of aerial duels in high-stakes matches.

## Practical Tips for Game Day

- **Identify Threats:** Before the match, analyze the opposition's key aerial threats and their tendencies.

- **Coordinate with Your Goalkeeper:** Ensure there's clear communication on who will challenge the ball and who will cover potential rebounds.

- **Stay Disciplined:** Avoid unnecessary fouls by maintaining clean physicality. Remember, a single foul in the penalty area can undo all your hard work.

By mastering these techniques and principles, you can transform from a reactive defender to a proactive one, turning set-piece threats into opportunities for your team.

Aerial battles are where defensive heroes emerge, especially during set pieces. Dominating these moments requires a blend of technical skill, physical preparedness, and unshakable confidence. Whether you're challenging a towering striker or meeting a lofted ball under pressure, success in the air is about more than just jumping—it's about precision, timing, and mindset.

## Defending Free Kicks: Walls, Positioning, and Concentration

Free kicks, whether direct or indirect, demand unparalleled discipline and awareness. A lapse in focus could easily lead to a goal.

## Understanding Direct vs. Indirect Free Kicks

**Direct Free Kick:** Awarded for severe fouls, these kicks allow the shooter to aim directly at the goal. Forming a defensive "wall" is crucial to protect the goal and limit the shooter's options.

*Example:* One of the most famous direct free kicks in history was Roberto Carlos' curling strike against France in 1997. The defensive wall was well-placed, but the shot's extraordinary bend and power caught everyone off guard—a reminder that even perfect positioning can sometimes fall
to brilliance.

## Indirect Free Kick:

Granted for less serious fouls, these require another player to touch the ball before a goal can count. Forming a "wall" here is equally important to protect the goal, as attackers often exploit defensive gaps with creative setups and dummy plays.

*Example:* In a 2019 Premier League match, Wolves scored an indirect free-kick goal against Leicester City by executing a deceptive short pass followed by a quick strike. The defense hesitated, momentarily confused by the setup, leaving space for the shot—a clear lesson on the importance of staying alert and organized.

## Building the Wall

The wall serves as the first line of defense against direct free
kicks. To be effective:

***Follow Your Goalkeeper's Instructions:*** The keeper positions the wall to block the most likely shooting angle.

***Stay Disciplined:*** Resist the urge to flinch or turn away. Jump only at the precise moment to block the ball.

***Project Confidence:*** A strong, unflinching wall can psychologically pressure the kicker.

**Real-Life Humor:** In an amateur game, a nervous defender turned his back and covered his face when the free kick was taken. The ball zipped past him into the goal, prompting his coach to shout:

*"Next time, wear a helmet!"*

**Why You Shouldn't Duck:**

The humor here underscores a critical point: the wall is only as effective as its defenders. Ducking or turning away creates gaps that skilled free-kick takers will exploit. Staying disciplined ensures the wall fulfills its purpose, blocking shots and reducing the angle for the kicker. A defender's confidence—or lack thereof—directly impacts their team's chances of stopping the goal. So, as funny as the "helmet" quip might be, it's a lighthearted reminder that bravery in the wall isn't just admirable—
it's essential!

**Maintaining Concentration in High-Pressure Moments**

Set pieces late in the game are the ultimate test of composure. Fatigue and pressure can make or break a defensive unit. Remaining calm and trusting your training is key.

**Dealing with Pressure**

Visualization is a powerful tool to help defenders mentally prepare for chaotic set-piece moments. Picture the scenario in your mind: the ball swinging into the penalty area, teammates holding their marks, and your decisive intervention. This mental rehearsal can build confidence and clarity.

To complement visualization, incorporate practical mental preparation techniques into your routine:

- **Controlled Breathing**: Before high-stakes moments, practice deep, steady breathing to calm nerves and sharpen focus. A simple method is inhaling for four counts, holding for four, and exhaling for four.

- **Pre-Game Rituals:** Develop habits that reinforce a focused mindset. Whether it's listening to a specific song, repeating a personal mantra, or running through a set of drills, these rituals can anchor your confidence.

- **Trust in Your Team:** Sharp communication ensures everyone executes their roles effectively. Keep instructions clear and concise, especially during high-pressure situations.

Combining these techniques helps you stay composed and proactive, turning the chaos of set pieces into an opportunity to excel.

*Real-Life Example:* In the 2005 Champions League final, AC Milan's lapse in concentration allowed Liverpool to equalize after trailing 3-0. This underscores how crucial focus is during high-pressure situations.

<h2 style="text-align:center">Visual Aid 4: High-Pressure Set Piece</h2>

## Conclusion: The Importance of Set-Piece Mastery

Defending set pieces is both an art and a science. These moments demand precision, strategy, and teamwork. From organizing teammates during corners to forming a disciplined wall in front of a free kick, set pieces test every aspect of a defender's skill.

Throughout history, the greatest defenders have excelled in these high-pressure situations. Legends like Paolo Maldini and Franz Beckenbauer made their mark by turning set-piece mastery into a defining element of their game. Their ability to organize, anticipate, and execute consistently under pressure set them apart.

As you progress on your defensive journey, remember that success in set pieces isn't just about clearing the ball. It's about thriving under pressure, trusting your teammates, and delivering when it matters most. Mastering these moments solidifies your place as a cornerstone of your team's defense and brings you closer to joining the ranks of the game's all-time greats.

- **Connecting Set Pieces to Life**
    Set pieces mirror the unpredictability and intensity of life's critical moments. The same qualities that define great defenders—discipline, focus, communication, perseverance, and resilience—are equally essential off the pitch.
- **Preparation Meets Opportunity**
    Just as defenders prepare for set pieces through training, success in life comes from preparation. Whether it's a job interview or a personal goal, planning leads to decisive action in critical moments.
- **Teamwork and Communication**
    Defenders rely on each other during set pieces. Similarly, life's toughest challenges often require collaboration and trust.
- **Resilience in High-Pressure Moments**
    Staying composed and disciplined under pressure, whether on the field or in life, often defines the outcome.

As you master the art of defending set pieces, take a moment to reflect on how these lessons apply to your everyday life.

## Memorable Takeaways (with Reflective Prompts)

Defending set pieces requires a blend of strategic planning, technical skill, and mental fortitude. The following takeaways encapsulate the essential lessons from this chapter, encouraging you to reflect on and apply these principles both on and off the pitch.

## Master Set-Piece Organization

*Key Insight:* Effective organization during set pieces—whether defending corners or free kicks—is crucial. Understanding and implementing zonal, man-marking, or hybrid systems ensures that your defense remains structured and responsive to the opponent's movements.

*Reflective Prompt:* How effectively does your team communicate and organize during set pieces?

What adjustments can you make to enhance your defensive organization in these high-pressure moments?

**Win the Aerial Duel with Precision and Confidence**

*Key Insight:* Dominating aerial battles is non-negotiable in set pieces. Success hinges on proper positioning, timing your jump, using your body to shield the ball, maintaining strong neck muscles, and having the confidence to win headers under pressure.

*Reflective Prompt:* Think of a recent aerial duel you were involved in. How did your positioning and timing influence the outcome? What specific techniques can you practice to improve your aerial dominance in future set pieces?

**Build a Disciplined and Effective Wall**

*Key Insight:* A well-constructed wall during direct free kicks can significantly reduce scoring opportunities. Discipline in following the goalkeeper's instructions, maintaining composure, and projecting confidence are key to forming an unyielding barrier.

*Reflective Prompt:* Reflect on a time when your defensive wall successfully thwarted a free kick. What aspects of your positioning and timing contributed to its effectiveness?

How can you further enhance your wall-building skills?

**Maintain Focus and Composure in High-Pressure Situations**

*Key Insight:* Set pieces, especially late in the game, test your mental toughness. Staying calm, trusting your training, and maintaining sharp communication are essential to executing your defensive duties effectively under pressure.

*Reflective Prompt:* Describe a high-pressure set-piece moment where you had to maintain composure. How did you manage your focus, and what strategies helped you stay calm and effective during that critical time?

## Enhance Communication and Coordination with Goalkeepers

*Key Insight:* Clear and constant communication with your goalkeeper is vital during set pieces. Coordinating who challenges the ball and who covers potential rebounds ensures that your defense operates as a unified unit, minimizing confusion and errors.

*Reflective Prompt:* How well do you communicate with your goalkeeper during set pieces? Identify any communication barriers you've encountered and propose ways to improve this crucial aspect of your defensive strategy.

## Develop Mental and Physical Resilience

*Key Insight:* Resilience is the cornerstone of effective defense during set pieces. Whether recovering from a missed clearance or maintaining intensity throughout the game, resilience ensures that you can handle setbacks and stay committed to your defensive responsibilities.

*Reflective Prompt:* Recall a moment during a set piece where resilience played a key role in your performance. How did you overcome the challenge, and what lessons can you apply to future high-pressure defensive situations?

## Utilize Training to Refine Set-Piece Skills

*Key Insight:* Consistent and targeted training is essential for mastering set-piece defense. Incorporating jumping and heading drills, reaction training, and strength conditioning into your routine builds the technical and physical foundation needed for success.

*Reflective Prompt:* Evaluate your current training regimen. Which specific drills have you found most effective for improving your set-piece defense, and what new training methods can you incorporate to further enhance your skills?

## Anticipate and Adapt to Opponent Strategies

*Key Insight:* Understanding and anticipating your opponent's set-piece strategies allows you to adapt your defensive approach accordingly.

Analyzing their tendencies and preparing specific responses can neutralize their threats before they materialize.

***Reflective Prompt:*** How do you prepare for the different set-piece strategies employed by your opponents? What steps can you take to better anticipate and counteract their specific tactics during corners and free kicks?

## Final Thought

**Mastering set-piece defense transforms chaotic moments into** controlled opportunities. By focusing on organization, aerial dominance, disciplined wall formation, and maintaining composure under pressure, you elevate your defensive game to new heights. These takeaways not only enhance your on-field performance but also instill valuable life skills such as teamwork, resilience, and strategic thinking.

As legendary defender Fabio Cannavaro once said, *"The secret to a strong defense is not just skill, but the will to stay organized, focused, and united under pressure."* Let this serve as your inspiration to approach every set piece with confidence and determination, turning challenges into triumphs.

## Summary and Bread Crumbs for Future Chapters

Set-piece mastery is the cornerstone of a great defense, blending mental and physical skills to overcome soccer's most chaotic moments.

In Chapter 6, we'll transition from defense to offense, exploring how defenders can turn a successful clearance into a counterattacking opportunity. The journey continues, and the lessons only deepen.

# CHAPTER 6: Possession and Transitions —The Power of Scanning and Turning Defense into Attack

**The Play That Changed It All**

In the 2019 UEFA Champions League semi-finals, Liverpool pulled off a miracle against Barcelona. One of the game's defining moments came not from a goal but from a split-second decision by Virgil van Dijk. With Barcelona surging forward, van Dijk intercepted a dangerous pass, scanned the field, and unleashed a precise ball to Trent Alexander-Arnold, triggering a swift counterattack. Seconds later, the ball was in the back of Barcelona's net. That one moment epitomized the power of scanning and transitions, turning defense into attack and changing the course of history.

This ability to process the game quickly is what separates elite defenders from the rest, and in this chapter, we'll break down how to develop this crucial skill. For defenders, scanning is more than looking around—it's the difference between survival and domination on the pitch.

**Introduction: The Art of Scanning and Transitioning**

Every great defender knows that winning the ball is only the beginning. The true magic lies in what happens next: transitioning from defense to attack. At the heart of this lies an often- overlooked skill—scanning.

Elite players like Lionel Messi scan the pitch an average of 6-8 times every 30 seconds, collecting information to make decisions in a split second. For defenders, the stakes are just as high. **As Pep Guardiola once said, _"It's not about how fast you move; it's about how fast you can see."_**

By mastering scanning, defenders not only improve their own decision-making but also enhance team cohesion, ensuring smoother transitions from defense to attack. This chapter unpacks the mechanics and importance of scanning, how it fuels possession, and how it transforms defenders into offensive catalysts.

**The Importance of Scanning: Awareness is Key**

Elite defenders don't just react—they anticipate. Scanning is the secret weapon that turns chaos into control. When defenders scan the field, they gather information about teammates, opponents, and spaces, empowering them to make smarter, faster decisions.

Greatness in soccer doesn't come from raw talent alone; it often hinges on intelligence and awareness. Scanning is one of the most defining skills that separate world-class players from merely good ones. Studies have consistently shown that players like Xavi Hernandez, Luka Modric, and Kevin De Bruyne scan the pitch far more frequently than others. This isn't a coincidence. Scanning enables them to anticipate situations, plan their next moves, and adapt instantly—before they even receive the ball.

While midfielders use scanning to orchestrate play, defenders rely on it to neutralize threats, predict opponent movements, and set up counterattacks. This distinction highlights how scanning is tailored to each position's unique demands, making it an indispensable skill across the pitch.

**Why Do Top Players Scan More?**

### 1.   They Think Ahead:

Elite players don't wait for the ball to dictate their actions.
By continuously scanning, they gain a three-dimensional understanding of their surroundings, allowing them to plan their first touch, next pass, or defensive adjustment.
This makes their movements efficient and purposeful.

### 2.   They Handle Pressure Better:

Pressure from opponents can fluster unprepared players. Frequent scanning reduces this anxiety by equipping players with options before they're under duress. This is particularly vital for defenders, who often operate in high-stakes areas where a single mistake can lead to a goal.

## 3.   They Read Patterns:

Regular scanning helps players notice repeating movements or tendencies in opponents. For example, a forward might always favor running to their left. Once a defender identifies this, they can neutralize the threat more effectively.

## 4.   They Exploit Weaknesses:

Scanning allows players to spot vulnerable areas in the opposition's formation. Whether it's a poorly positioned defender or an unmarked teammate, this awareness creates opportunities that others might miss.

### Real-Life Example: Xavi Hernandez

At Barcelona, Xavi was known to scan the pitch up to 12 times in the 10 seconds before receiving the ball. This extraordinary frequency gave him an almost supernatural ability to control games, making him the engine of one of soccer's greatest teams.

*"The more information you have, the better decisions you can make. Before the ball gets to me, I already know what I'm going to do with it."*
*— Xavi Hernandez*

By understanding the value of scanning, defenders can transform themselves into decision-makers who guide the rhythm of the game.

**Scanning Options for Defenders without the Ball** Even off the ball, scanning shows awareness and anticipation:

### Opponent Movement

***Look for Threats Behind***: Regularly check over your shoulder for forwards making sneaky runs behind the defensive line.

***Monitor Patterns***: Observe attacking players' positioning during quick transitions or set pieces to predict their next moves.

## Teammate Positioning

***Spot Defensive Support***: Locate nearby teammates to maintain compact coverage or support clearances.

***Assess Passing Options***: Identify outlets like midfielders or full-backs for safe possession plays.

## Ball Progression

***Watch the Ball Carrier***: Track the opponent with the ball to anticipate their intentions.

***Predict Passing Lanes***: Read the game to intercept or position effectively.

## Space Awareness

***Identify Open Spaces***: Recognize areas for interceptions or for teammates to exploit during counterattacks.

***Anticipate Danger Zones***: Spot spaces the opponent could use to turn the game against you.

Imagine a defender facing a high press—by scanning early, they can spot an open full-back for a quick switch of play, avoiding unnecessary turnovers.

This proactive approach not only diffuses immediate threats but also sets the stage for a smoother transition from defense to attack.

A. Intended receiver #11 making diagonal run behind central
defender #5.
Central defender scans movement of potential receiver.

B. Central defender anticipates the pass from scanning and
positions himself to intercept the ball.

**C.  Central defender steps forward and intercepts the pass.**

## Why Scanning Matters for Defenders

- **Anticipation:** Know what's happening before it happens.
- **Retention:** Avoid turnovers by acting with purpose.
- **Transitions:** Seamlessly shift from defense to offense.

## Real-Life Inspiration: Messi and Van Dijk

- **Lionel Messi:** Renowned for his scanning, Messi uses information to make razor- sharp decisions, exploiting every inch of space.
- **Virgil van Dijk:** A master of defensive scanning, van Dijk combines awareness with composure to launch attacks with pinpoint precision.
- **Scanning and Possession**: The Calm before the Counterattack

Regaining possession is only the first step; keeping it is what counts. Defenders who scan effectively can secure the ball and dictate the next move, whether it's a short, composed pass or a long, aggressive clearance.

## Short Passes vs. Long Passes

- **Short Passes**: Build control and regroup the team. For example, when under pressure, a center-back may opt for a short pass to a midfielder to retain possession and reset the play.
- **Long Passes**: Exploit gaps and kick start counterattacks. A well-placed long diagonal ball can be more effective when exploiting an opponent's high line, quickly transitioning the team into an attacking opportunity.

Understanding when to choose between these options is essential for maintaining balance between defensive stability and offensive ambition.

**Real-Life Example: Barcelona's Possession Play**

Gerard Piqué, under Guardiola's guidance, mastered scanning for short passes to Sergio Busquets, creating controlled build-ups that evolved into devastating attacks.

## Visual Aid 2: Goal Keeper Scanning for Quick Distribution to Viable Options

## The Transition: Turning Defense into Attack

The best defenders don't just stop attacks; they start them. Scanning accelerates transitions, exploiting the opponent's disorganization after losing possession.

## Keys to Effective Transitions

- **Quick Decisions:** Speed destabilizes the opposition.

- **Exploiting Space:** Scanning reveals the openings that make transitions lethal. In a *4-3-3 setup*, quick transitions can exploit wide spaces, stretching the defense and creating 1v1 situations on the flanks. Meanwhile, a *3-5-2 formation* may focus more on central overloads, using quick vertical passes to break lines and overwhelm the opposition in the middle of the field.

## Real-Life Example: Raphaël Varane

In Real Madrid's 2020 campaign, Varane's ability to scan and find teammates in space turned defense into high-quality attacks, bypassing entire defensive lines.

*Humor Break*: A lower-league defender was scanning so frantically during a match that his teammates joked, "Are you searching for a passing option or your lost keys?" The coach laughed: "Focus on marking first, scanning second—we're already down two goals!"

The humor in this anecdote serves to highlight the balance required when scanning on the pitch. While scanning is a critical skill, overdoing it— especially without prioritizing immediate defensive responsibilities— can be counterproductive.

**Here's the underlying point:**

- Scanning enhances awareness and decision-making, but it should not come at the cost of neglecting primary defensive duties, such as marking opponents or maintaining structure.
- The joke illustrates how even an important skill like scanning can become a distraction if not applied with the right focus and timing.

It uses lightheartedness to remind players to prioritize their immediate role in defending while integrating scanning as a complementary skill.

### Goalkeeper's Role in Transitions

Modern goalkeepers, like Ederson and Neuer, are pivotal in transitions. Their scanning and distribution break defensive lines before the opposition can react.

### Training for Scanning and Distribution

One effective drill involves goalkeepers making rapid decisions under pressure. They receive passes from various angles and must distribute the ball within three seconds, replicating game-like scenarios where quick thinking and precise execution are essential for launching counterattacks.

### Real-Life Example: Neuer's Swift Distribution

Manuel Neuer's scanning and quick throws repeatedly catch opponents off guard, launching Bayern Munich into blistering counterattacks.

**Humor Break:** *After Neuer's throw led to a goal, the opposing coach joked, "We didn't even have time to realize who had the ball!"*

### Conclusion: Scanning and Transitioning— A Defender's Superpower

By mastering scanning, defenders don't just react—they dictate the game. This skill enhances anticipation, safeguards possession, and triggers quick transitions, proving that defense is the foundation of attack. Whether you're a full-back looking for overlaps or a center-back anticipating a striker's run, scanning shapes both defensive awareness and offensive contribution, making it an indispensable tool for modern defenders.

## Beyond the Pitch

Scanning isn't just a skill for the soccer field—it's a mindset for life. In both sports and everyday situations, awareness and the ability to anticipate can make a critical difference.

## Why Scanning Is a Life Skill

- **Enhanced Decision-Making**:

Just like in soccer, life often presents you with fleeting opportunities that demand quick, informed decisions. Whether it's seizing a career opening or responding to a personal challenge, the ability to assess your environment is invaluable.

- **Better Problem-Solving:**

Players' scan to identify passing lanes, open spaces, or threats; similarly, in life, scanning can help individuals identify solutions to complex problems. Awareness of surroundings, people, and situations fosters innovative thinking and proactive behavior.

- **Improved Communication**:

On the pitch, scanning is often followed by communication—calling out to a teammate or organizing a defensive line. Off the pitch, this skill translates into strong interpersonal communication, whether in leadership roles or collaborative environments. In business and strategic decision-making, professionals who constantly assess market trends, team dynamics, and emerging challenges can anticipate shifts and act decisively, much like a player reading the game before making a move.

## Real-Life Parallel: Entrepreneurs and Leaders

Business leaders like Tim Cook CEO of Apple Inc., or Indra Nooyi CEO and Chairperson of PepsiCo are masters of "scanning" their environments. They constantly gather information from the market, their teams, and emerging trends, enabling them to adapt swiftly and steer their companies in the right direction.

**Practical Exercise: Applying Scanning in Daily Life**

- **Step 1:** Choose an environment where decisions are frequent—such as meetings, classrooms, or even while driving.

- **Step 2:** Make a conscious effort to observe everything around you. What patterns do you notice? Are there opportunities or risks you hadn't considered before?

- **Step 3:** Use this awareness to make better-informed decisions. For example, in a meeting, proactively address an issue before it becomes a problem.

By viewing scanning as a universal skill, players can take what they've learned on the field and apply it to their personal and professional lives, turning situational awareness into a powerful advantage.

**Memorable Takeaways (with Reflective Prompts)**

1. **Scanning is Essential**
   - **Takeaway:** Constant scanning improves decision-making.
   - **Prompt:** How can you train your eyes to always stay one step ahead?
2. **Maintain Possession Under Pressure**
   - **Takeaway:** Calm defenders reduce turnovers.
   - **Prompt:** What techniques help you stay composed when under pressure?
3. **Transition Quickly**
   - **Takeaway:** Fast transitions destabilize opponents.
   - **Prompt:** How can you improve your reaction speed after regaining possession?

4. **Goalkeepers Are Key Partners**
   - **Takeaway:** Goalkeepers' distribution can transform defense into offense.

- Prompt: How can you coordinate better with your goalkeeper?

5. **Scanning as a Lifelong Skill**

- **Takeaway:** Scanning builds both soccer IQ and life adaptability.
- **Prompt:** How can you practice being more aware of your surroundings in daily situations, such as during a conversation or while problem-solving?

## Summary and Bread Crumbs for Future Chapters

This chapter emphasized the power of scanning and transitions, showing how awareness shapes the game's rhythm.
The examples from Messi, van Dijk, and Neuer illuminated how this skill transforms players into playmakers.

In the next chapter, we'll explore Defensive Leadership and Communication, delving into how organizing teammates and commanding the backline elevate individual and team performance.

# CHAPTER 7: Defensive Leadership and Communication —The Voice That Commands

## A Voice That Saved the Match

During the 2006 World Cup, Italy faced Germany in a nail-biting semi-final. With just minutes left in extra time, Fabio Cannavaro, Italy's legendary captain, shouted instructions to his defenders and midfielders, reorganizing the entire team in a matter of seconds. His leadership and composure paved the way for Italy to win the ball, initiate a counterattack, and secure a place in the final. Cannavaro's voice didn't just direct—it commanded, inspired, and ultimately, saved the match.

This moment exemplifies how leadership is not just about individual brilliance, but about orchestrating the entire defensive unit to act with purpose and precision. Defensive leadership is more than tactics; it's about presence. In this chapter, we uncover how elite defenders like Cannavaro, John Terry, and Paolo Maldini use their voices and vision to guide their teams to victory.

## Introduction: The Heart of Defensive Leadership

Great defending isn't just about blocking shots—it's about leading from the back. Elite defenders organize the defensive line, anticipate danger, and ensure everyone is in sync. They are the team's backbone, combining tactical acumen with vocal authority.

As John Terry famously said, *"In defense, communication is everything. It's about knowing your role and making sure everyone else knows theirs."* While some players possess natural leadership qualities, effective communication and defensive organization are skills that can be refined through training and experience. This chapter explores the art of defensive leadership and communication, showing how organizing the backline, vocal commands, and mental composure elevate defenders from good to great.

## Organizing the Backline and Commanding the Field

A solid defense functions like a well-oiled machine, with every player moving as one. Effective organization is critical, and defensive leaders are the architects of this unity. Great defenders position themselves strategically, directing teammates to close gaps, maintain offside traps, and stay alert to threats.

**As Franz Beckenbauer once said,** *"A good defense is like a wall—solid, unbreakable, and unified."*

### Key Principles of Defensive Organization

The defensive organization is the foundation of any great backline. It ensures defenders work as a unified unit, making it difficult for opponents to exploit spaces. The following principles form the bedrock of defensive success, progressing logically from maintaining structure to reacting dynamically in transitions:

### Compactness in Action

Compactness is about minimizing space between defenders and midfielders, forcing attackers into wide or congested areas where they are less effective. When the defensive line moves as a unit—both laterally and vertically—it minimizes exploitable gaps. For example, Paolo Maldini's AC Milan suffocated opposition attacks by maintaining tight spacing and sharp positional adjustments.

*Practical Tip*: Communicate constantly with your teammates to keep the line intact. Use phrases like "Tighten up!" to maintain cohesion during transitions.

### Positional Awareness in Action

Defenders must understand their role in the setup and adjust their position based on the flow of play. Positional awareness involves reading the game and positioning yourself strategically to cover spaces and track runners. Sergio Ramos exemplified this by cutting off passing lanes while being ready to cover gaps left by advancing full-backs.

***Practical Tip***: Practice regularly checking over your shoulder and scanning the field to stay aware of your position relative to your teammates
and opponents.

## Cohesion in Action

A cohesive defensive unit moves together like a single entity. If one player steps up or drops back without coordination, it can create exploitable gaps. Cohesion becomes critical during set pieces or when holding a high defensive line, as seen in Liverpool's well-drilled backline under Virgil
van Dijk.

***Practical Tip***: Train with drills that require synchronized movements, such as stepping up to execute an offside trap or retreating to defend as a line during a counterattack. Vocal cues like *"Hold!"* or *"Push up!"* ensure everyone is on the same page. Modern teams use technology like GPS tracking and video analysis to refine defensive positioning and ensure optimal organization, allowing defenders to analyze movement patterns and improve real-time decision-making.

## Anticipation in Action

Anticipation allows defenders to neutralize threats before they develop. This means reading the game, predicting opponents' movements, and timing interceptions or tackles perfectly. Giorgio Chiellini is renowned for anticipating both the ball's trajectory and the opposition's intent, neutralizing threats before they could materialize.

***Practical Tip***: Study your opponents' patterns and habits. In practice, focus on small-sided games to improve your ability to read plays and make
quick decisions.

## Transition Readiness in Action

Defensive transitions test a team's ability to adapt. Whether shifting to attack after regaining possession or reorganizing to defend after losing it, transitions require discipline and communication. Spain's 2010 World Cup-winning team showcased this by maintaining compactness during counterattacks, preventing opponents from exploiting
disorganized gaps.

***Practical Tip:*** Rehearse quick defensive-to-offensive transitions in training, emphasizing compactness and clear communication to avoid breakdowns.

## Visual Aid 1: Tactical Unity: Commanding the Backline through Movement and Communication

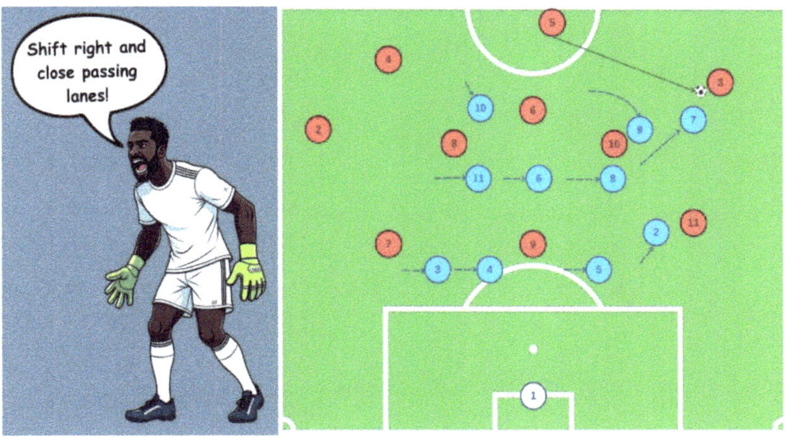


## Real-Life Example: Maldini's Mastery

Paolo Maldini's leadership at AC Milan exemplified defensive organization. Whether orchestrating the offside trap or marking a dangerous forward, Maldini's ability to read the game and command his teammates set him apart as a defensive maestro.

## Vocal Leadership: Making Yourself Heard

A defender's voice is as critical as their tackle. Vocal leaders issue concise, impactful commands, ensuring clarity and focus across the defensive unit.

**Simple, Effective Communication**

- ***Concise Commands***: Use short, actionable phrases like "Hold!" "Step up!" or "Mark!"

- ***Encouragement***: Positive reinforcement keeps teammates focused and confident, e.g., "Well done!" or "Stay sharp!"

- ***Alerts***: Signal danger with urgency, like shouting "Man on!" or "Watch the run!"

A real-game example of effective communication can be seen in the 2018 World Cup, where France's Raphaël Varane and Hugo Lloris consistently coordinated positioning and responsibilities. Their clear instructions and vocal leadership helped prevent defensive lapses, ensuring France remained compact and organized on their way to winning the tournament.

**Real-Life Example: Terry's Decisive Voice**

John Terry's vocal leadership at Chelsea kept the backline disciplined. Whether organizing set-piece marking or directing play under pressure, Terry's voice was a constant presence, guiding his team to defensive excellence.

**Humor Break: Leadership with a Laugh**

During one high-pressure match, a defender yelled, *"We're playing defense like we've got Wi-Fi, and the attackers have the password!"* The humor diffused the tension, allowing the team to refocus and tighten up their game.

**Beyond the Backline: Leading the Whole Field**

Defensive leaders don't stop at organizing their line—they extend their influence to midfielders, full-backs, and even the goalkeeper.

## Guiding Midfielders and Full-Backs

- **Midfield Shielding:** Signal midfielders to drop back or press high, depending on the situation.
- **Full-Back Positioning:** Ensure full-backs strike a balance between attack and defense, preventing gaps on the flanks.

## Partnering with the Goalkeeper

Defensive leaders and goalkeepers must work as one, especially during set pieces and transitions. The goalkeeper's view of the field often makes them an essential ally in organizing the backline. However, a defender may take control at times based on his leadership ability.

Effective leaders not only rely on their voice but also use hand signals and body positioning to guide teammates without verbal commands. A raised hand can indicate an offside trap, a pointed finger can direct marking assignments, and an open palm can signal calmness under pressure. These nonverbal cues ensure clarity, especially in loud stadiums where verbal communication may be lost.

**Visual Aid 2: Extending Leadership Beyond the Backline**

**Humor from the Goalkeeper's Box**

**After a scramble during a corner, Manuel Neuer once quipped, *"Am I the goalkeeper or the team babysitter?"* The humor helped ease tension while reinforcing the need for organization**.

**The Mental Aspect of Leadership: Calm under Pressure**

The best leaders don't just command—they inspire composure.

Staying calm during high-pressure moments prevents panic and reduces mistakes.

**"Composure is Contagious"**

When a defensive leader maintains composure, it sets the tone for the entire team. Composure is about controlling emotions, staying focused, and making rational decisions under pressure. This mental calmness prevents panic during high-stress situations, like defending a slim lead in the final minutes of a match.

A composed defender sends a powerful, unspoken message to teammates: "We've got this." For example, when Vincent Kompany led Manchester City's defense, his poise in crunch moments inspired confidence in his teammates, even during high-stakes matches like the 2012 Premier League finale.

**Practical ways to develop composure include:**

- **Mental Visualization:** Rehearse high-pressure scenarios mentally before games.

- **Controlled Breathing:** Practice deep-breathing exercises to reduce stress during tense moments.

- **Focus Drills:** Train concentration by reacting to unpredictable movements or sounds in practice.

Composure also influences the crowd and opponents. A calm demeanor can diffuse tense atmospheres while visibly rattled players energize opposition teams. Leaders like Cannavaro and Maldini knew how to project confidence, which rippled across their squad and created a sense of unshakable unity.

A prime example of composure under pressure was seen in the **2012 Champions League final**, where **Chelsea's defense remained resolute** despite relentless Bayern Munich attacks. Through disciplined organization and unwavering focus, they forced the game into penalties, where their composure ultimately secured victory.

**Reflective Prompt**

What specific techniques can you use to project calmness and instill confidence in your teammates?

**Visual Aid 3: Leadership Under Pressure:
Calmness Creates Confidence.**

**Real-Life Example: Chelsea's 2012 Champions League Final**

In the dying moments of the final, Chelsea's defense, led by Terry, stayed calm despite Bayern Munich's relentless pressure. Their composure helped force penalties, where Chelsea ultimately triumphed.

**Conclusion: Leadership as the Cornerstone of Defense**

Defensive leadership is the foundation of great defending. From organizing the backline to inspiring confidence through vocal commands and mental composure, leaders like Terry, Maldini, and Cannavaro show that the best defenders lead with both their minds and voices.

True defensive leaders aren't born—they are built through experience, discipline, and the ability to lift those around them.

Every match, every challenge, and every moment of adversity is an opportunity to refine these qualities and become the backbone of a team.

## Leadership beyond the Game

Defensive leadership teaches skills that transcend soccer. Clear communication, calmness under pressure, and the ability to guide others are invaluable in any leadership role, whether on the pitch, in the office, or life.

## Memorable Takeaways (with Reflective Prompts)

1. **Organize to Dominate:** Clear defensive organization stops attacks before they start.
   - *Prompt:* How can I better communicate positioning to my teammates?
2. **Communicate Clearly:** Simple, concise commands ensure clarity under pressure.
   - *Prompt:* What key phrases can I use to improve communication on the field?
3. **Calmness is Key:** Composure inspires confidence across the team.
   - *Prompt:* How do I stay mentally strong in high-pressure situations?
4. **Extend Your Influence:** True leaders guide beyond their position.
   - *Prompt:* How can I better support my midfielders and goalkeeper?
5. **Humor in Leadership:** Light moments keep the team focused and united.
   - *Prompt:* When can humor help ease tension and refocus the team?

## Summary and Bread Crumbs for Future Chapters

This chapter explored defensive leadership as the backbone of a strong team, focusing on communication, organization, and composure. In Chapter 8, we'll shift to Defensive Resilience and Adaptability, examining how defenders adjust to challenges like tactical changes, injuries, and high-pressure scenarios. Mastering adaptability will take your defensive skills to the next level.

# CHAPTER 8: Defensive Resilience and Adaptability—Overcoming Challenges on the Field

**Thriving in the Eye of the Storm**

**Think About This Image**

It's the 75th minute of a high-stakes final. Your team is down to ten men, the opposition is piling on the pressure, and the crowd is roaring. The air is charged with tension, and every move feels like a gamble.

It's here, in the chaos, that legends are born. Great defenders don't just survive these moments—they thrive, staying composed, adapting to shifting tactics, and inspiring their team to hold the line. Their ability to remain calm under pressure and make intelligent decisions defines their leadership.

Composure and adaptability are what separate elite defenders from the rest. Whether it's adjusting to a tactical change, reading the game's momentum, or leading by example, these moments test everything a defender has trained for.

**The question is, can you rise to the occasion?**

**Introduction: Resilience and Adaptability— The DNA of Great Defenders**

Defensive resilience and adaptability are the hallmarks of elite defenders. Injuries, red cards, and tactical surprises are inevitable in soccer, but what separates the good from the great is the ability to rise above these challenges.

As Gary Cahill reflected after Chelsea's improbable 2012 Champions League victory, *"It wasn't just about defending; it was about staying calm when the whole world was watching."*

Maintaining composure in high-pressure moments requires more than just natural ability—it demands mental toughness, tactical awareness, and the ability to make split-second decisions under stress. In this chapter, we delve into the mindset, strategies, and real-life examples that showcase how defenders overcome adversity and shine when it matters most.

## Maintaining Composure in Adverse Situations: Thriving When the Odds Are Against You

### The Power of Composure

As Chunyi Lin reflects in *Born a Healer*, *"In the quiet moments of stillness, the greatest truths reveal themselves. Embrace calmness as your guide."* This wisdom captures the essence of defensive composure. In the heat of the game, calmness allows defenders to assess situations clearly, respond decisively, and inspire stability within their team. It is in these quiet, composed moments that defenders see the game's bigger picture and act with precision rather than panic.

Like any skill, composure under pressure can be trained. Controlled pressure drills simulate high-intensity moments, helping defenders develop the ability to stay calm and make the right decisions. However, no matter the situation, one key principle remains constant:

### Stick to the Fundamentals

Even under extreme pressure, elite defenders rely on the basics—staying compact, marking tightly, and forcing opponents into low-percentage shots. These core principles keep the defense structured and difficult to break down, regardless of adversity.

- **Small-Sided Pressing Drills:** Defenders must play out from the back under relentless pressure, improving their ability to remain composed while making quick, accurate decisions.

- **Reduced Time and Space Games:** Training with limited touches and smaller playing areas forces defenders to stay focused and execute under tight conditions.
- **Breath Control and Visualization:** Practicing deep breathing techniques and mentally rehearsing high-pressure scenarios strengthens a player's ability to manage stress in real-time situations.

By combining mental composure with defensive fundamentals, defenders can stay in control even in chaotic moments, ensuring they react with clarity rather than emotion when the game demands it most.

**Visual Aid 1: Defending with Nine Players:
Compact and Disciplined Defense**

**Key Takeaway: Calm Leads to Clarity**

In adversity, defensive leaders must exude calm, providing direction that keeps teammates focused. Panic spreads quickly, but so does composure. When a defender remains composed, it reassures the team, allowing for clear decision-making and structured play, even under pressure.

*Reflection Prompt:* Think about a high-pressure moment you've faced—on or off the pitch. How did you react? Did you bring calm to the situation, or did emotions take over? What could you do differently next time to maintain clarity and control?

By practicing composure and self-awareness, players can develop the leadership qualities that turn tense moments into opportunities
for greatness.

**Adapting to Tactical Shifts: Flexibility is Key**

**Reading and Reacting in Real-Time**

Tactical flexibility separates great defenders from the rest. Whether it's a sudden switch to two strikers or the introduction of a long-ball tactic, quick recognition and adjustment prevent lapses in defense.

Adjusting marking responsibilities in real time requires constant scanning, clear communication, and quick decision-making.
When the opposition alters positioning—such as switching formations or overloading one side—defenders must:

- **Communicate instantly**: Use verbal cues like "Switch!" or "Tighten up!" to reassign marking duties.
- **Maintain compact shape**: Shift as a unit to close passing lanes and prevent gaps.
- **Adapt roles dynamically**: A center-back may need to step up, while a full-back tucks inside to cover.

By staying **alert and vocal**, defenders can seamlessly adjust, keeping defensive structure intact despite tactical shifts.

## Key Principle: Adapt Marking Responsibilities

When a team shifts tactics, defenders must communicate adjustments, ensuring every threat is accounted for.

## Real-Life Example

In the Euro 2012 final, Spain's quick transitions forced Italy's defenders to constantly readjust their positioning. The ability to adapt kept Spain in control, showcasing tactical mastery.

## Humor in Action

During a Sunday league match, a tactical switch prompted a confused defender to shout, "Are we parking the bus or driving it off a cliff?!" Moments like this highlight the importance of clarity in adapting to change.

**Visual Aid 2: Defending Team Adapting to Opponent's Changes: Adjusting Marking Responsibilities**

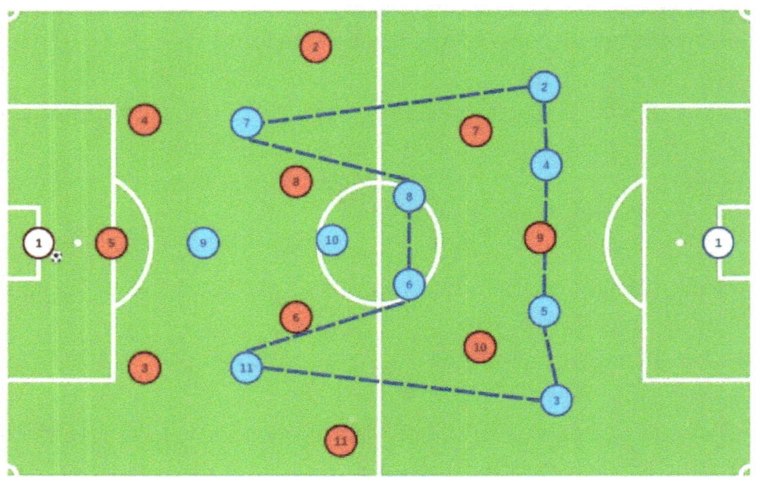

**Attacking Team Playing with One Striker (#9)**

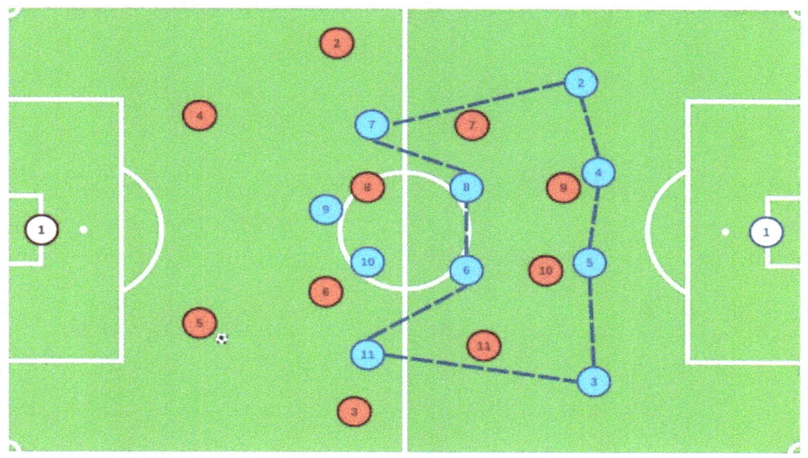

**Attacking Team Playing with Two Strikers (#9 & #10)**

## Responding to Injuries and Disruptions

## Rising to the Occasion

Injuries disrupt defensive structure and morale. Resilient defenders take on added responsibilities, ensuring the team doesn't lose its shape.

## Key Principle: Next Player up Mentality

Every defender must be ready to step into a new role when a teammate is injured or subbed out unexpectedly. Versatility isn't just an asset—it's a necessity at the highest level.

## Real-Life Example

During the 2018 World Cup, Benjamin Pavard stepped into an unfamiliar role for France due to injuries, delivering a stunning performance—and scoring a crucial goal. His adaptability and composure under pressure proved invaluable to his team's success.

**How to Prepare for Unexpected Positional Changes**

*Tactical Awareness*: Study multiple positions within your defensive setup to understand responsibilities beyond your primary role.

*Physical Readiness*: Train in various defensive movements—covering wide spaces as a full-back, stepping into midfield as a center-back, or even playing in a back three.

*Mental Resilience*: Embrace unpredictability by simulating in-game role changes during training, forcing quick adjustments in marking and positioning.

By developing adaptability in both mindset and skill set, defenders ensure they can rise to the challenge whenever the team calls on them.

*Humor in Tough Moments:* After a center-back injury in an amateur game, a nervous midfielder stepped into the role, muttering, "I've never been this far back... hope I don't get a nosebleed!" Humor lightened the mood and kept the team focused.

**Defensive Unity: Weathering the Storm Together**

**Resilience: A Collective Effort**

Resilience isn't just about individual effort—it's about the entire defensive unit standing together. Trust and constant communication are the glue that holds defenses together during adversity.

**Key Principle: Compactness is Key**

A compact defensive shape reduces gaps, forces attackers wide, and ensures every defender has support.

**Real-Life Example**

Porto's disciplined defense under José Mourinho in the 2004 Champions League final exemplified unity. They stayed compact, trusted each other, and secured the title by neutralizing Monaco's attacking threats.

**Knowing Teammates' Tendencies**

Familiarity with teammates' habits—like a full-back's preference to push forward—allows defenders to anticipate and cover seamlessly, maintaining structural integrity.

**Practical Drill: Defensive Synchronization**

***Drill Name****: Shadow Movement Defense*

Form a back four or back five in training.

- A coach or attacking players shift the ball across the field, simulating offensive movements.
- Defenders move as a unit, adjusting compactness and spacing while maintaining clear communication.
- Add random triggers, such as a full-back pushing forward or a center-back stepping up, forcing defenders to adjust instinctively.

This drill builds trust, sharpens positioning awareness, and reinforces defensive cohesion, ensuring defenders react instinctively under real-game pressure.

## Conclusion: Rising Above Adversity

Great defenders are forged in moments of adversity. Injuries, red cards, and tactical shifts reveal their character. The best defenders keep their composure, adapt to any situation, and inspire their teammates to rise alongside them. By embracing these challenges, defenders transform adversity into defining moments of leadership and resilience.

## Resilience beyond the Field

The lessons of defensive resilience echo far beyond the boundaries of a soccer pitch. Life, much like the game, is unpredictable. You'll face injuries to your plans, sudden tactical shifts in your goals, and moments where the odds feel stacked against you. How you respond in these moments defines your character.

a. *Adaptability Creates Opportunity*: Embracing change with agility and focus turns challenges into chances for growth.

b.  ***Unity in Adversity***: Trusting and leaning on your team—whether friends, family, or colleagues—helps weather life's storms.

c.  ***Calm in the Chaos***: Maintaining composure under pressure paves the way for clear decisions, even in the most turbulent times.

Resilience is not just a skill; it's a way of life. By embodying the adaptability, composure, and unity of great defenders, you can tackle challenges head-on, both on the field and beyond. When life's chaos tests you, remember: the calm amid the storm is where greatness thrives.

**Memorable Takeaways (with Reflective Prompts)**

a.  **Adaptability is Essential**

Adjust to sudden changes without losing focus or structure. ***Reflective Prompt***: Think about a time when a sudden change impacted your role on the team. How did you adapt, and what did you learn from the experience?

b.  **Composure in Crisis**

Staying calm leads to better decisions and stronger defenses. ***Reflective Prompt***: What strategies help you remain composed under pressure?

c.  **Trust Your Teammates**

Defensive unity thrives on trust and communication. ***Reflective Prompt***: How can you build stronger trust within your defensive line?

d.  **Lead Through Adversity**

Leadership in tough moments ensures the team stays cohesive. ***Reflective Prompt***: Have you taken on unexpected leadership in challenging moments? What impact did it have?

**Summary and Bread Crumbs for Future Chapters**

This chapter illustrated how defenders rise above adversity through resilience, adaptability, and unity. Whether managing tactical shifts, playing with nine or ten men, or stepping up after injuries, these moments define the greats. Defensive adaptability isn't just about survival—it's about control. The best defenders don't merely react to chaos; they use their awareness and decision-making to shape the game's flow, dictating when to slow the tempo or accelerate transitions.

In Chapter 9, we'll explore how elite defenders go beyond preventing goals to influence the match's rhythm. By mastering control from the backline, they become more than just stoppers—they become the architects of the game.
Stay tuned for the next step in mastering defense.

# CHAPTER 9: Controlling the Game from the Backline—Dictating the Tempo and Pacing the Match

Envision this scene: the game is in full swing, and the crowd is locked in a frenzy. Amid the chaos, a single figure at the backline takes charge—not through dazzling dribbles or flashy goals, but with quiet authority. Every pass they make shifts the game's tempo, every shout organizes the team, and every decision redirects the flow of play. This is the defender as a conductor, dictating the match's rhythm and ensuring that control starts from the back. It's not about reacting to the game—it's about owning it.

This foundational role is pivotal to the backline's strategic influence in pacing the game. By mastering timing and precision, defenders set the stage for transitions, turning defense into a Launchpad for attack. Their vision and composure ripple through the team, forging a unified strategy that balances aggression with control, ensuring that the game remains theirs to command.

## Introduction: The Backline as the Heartbeat of the Game

Defense is often perceived as reactive, a response to the threat of attack. But the truth is far more compelling: defenders have the power to dictate how the game unfolds. Whether through precise communication, calculated tempo shifts, or split-second decision-making, elite defenders wield influence that stretches far beyond the backline.

From Carles Puyol's calm control under pressure to Virgil van Dijk's commanding leadership, this chapter uncovers how defenders use intelligence, composure, and foresight to transform games. Just as a point guard in basketball dictates the offense, a defender in soccer dictates the game's rhythm. The backline becomes the heartbeat of the team, ensuring that both order and opportunity arise from even the most chaotic moments.

Controlling the tempo is more than just technical skill; it's a mindset, a form of game intelligence that distinguishes elite defenders. As we journey through this chapter, think of defending not as a reactive stance but as an active form of game management, where the backline isn't just a wall but a well-oiled machine.

And yes, sometimes it feels like you're steering the ship while yelling at a ball to "Stay in play!"

For example, consider a pivotal moment during the 2014 World Cup quarterfinal between the Netherlands and Costa Rica. Dutch defender Ron Vlaar showcased impeccable tempo control by holding the backline steady and calmly recycling possession under immense pressure from Costa Rica's aggressive pressing. By consistently switching play and maintaining composure, Vlaar dictated the rhythm of the match, preventing Costa Rica from capitalizing on their quick transitions. This disciplined control allowed the Netherlands to weather the storm and eventually triumph in the penalty shootout.

Such scenarios highlight how a defender's ability to control the tempo transforms them from mere players into orchestrators of the game's flow. This mastery of tempo feeds directly into the practical elements of game pacing—knowing when to slow the game down to regain control or accelerate it to catch the opponent off guard.
The next section will delve into these tactics, providing actionable insights to apply this skill effectively.

**Commanding the Tempo—Pacing the Match to Your Advantage**

A great defender controls the rhythm of the game, whether holding a narrow lead or countering relentless attacks. Shifting the pace can frustrate the opponent, rally teammates, and ultimately tilt the match in your favor.

**a.** **Slowing Down the Game by Passing to Goal Keeper or Faking an Injury**

**b.** **Speeding Up the Game by Passing the Ball Up the Field**

**Slowing the Game Down**

When you're under pressure, a savvy defender might pass the ball back to the keeper, holding it just long enough to reset the team's shape. Slowing the game is like pulling back in a chess match—strategic, calming, and, for your opponents, infuriating. As legendary Spanish defender Carles Puyol demonstrated in the 2010 World Cup, patience is a defender's virtue. His team held their lead by calmly working the ball, controlling possession, and waiting for their moment to strike.

For instance, Italy's defensive control in the Euro 2020 final against England serves as a modern testament to this principle.
Trailing early in the game, Italy's backline, led by Leonardo Bonucci and Giorgio Chiellini, deliberately slowed the pace, using calculated passes to diffuse England's high-energy attacks.

This composure allowed Italy to regain their footing, equalize, and eventually win in a penalty shootout.

Imagine trying to get young players to stay calm under pressure. You might tell them to visualize a "pause button" in their heads, giving them an internal moment to regroup when things heat up. That pause can make all the difference in finding your footing and setting up your next move.

- **Speeding it up — The Quick Transition**

When the opportunity presents itself, defenders can also crank up the speed. Winning the ball and immediately launching a forward pass can catch opponents off guard, creating a swift counterattack. As Franz Beckenbauer, the "Kaiser" of defense, often demonstrated, the element of surprise is key. His quick transitions from defense to attack left opponents scrambling to react.

Think of it like flipping a switch—one moment, the game is steady; the next, it's electric. A well-timed play can propel the team into attacking mode, shifting the game's entire momentum in seconds. This ability to read the situation and execute with precision transforms a defender from a stopper to a catalyst for scoring opportunities.

## Orchestrating the Defense Leadership through Communication

Great defenders don't just throw in tackles; they communicate constantly, organizing teammates, adjusting lines, and reading the opponent's intentions.

Every shout, gesture, or nudge is part of a greater orchestration, with defenders acting as the game's *"traffic cops,"* minus the shiny whistles (though sometimes we wish we had those, too).

## Controlling the Midfield from the Back

Defenders keep a close eye on their midfielders, ensuring they don't let anyone sneak by unmarked.

A high line, for example, forces the opposition into tighter spaces, restricting their movement.

However, if the midfield is too high, defenders may find themselves with no cover at all—cue a defender's worst nightmare.

***Actionable Takeaway***: Constant communication with your midfield is essential. In training, work on coordinated positioning drills that help you and your midfielders adjust dynamically. This balance not only closes down space but also ensures that when the high line is pressed, there's always adequate cover behind.

**Take Virgil van Dijk at Liverpool.** His command over his teammates goes beyond simply telling them to "watch the runner." His voice becomes the glue that keeps the entire line in sync, turning chaos into order with a quick shout. This kind of communication—constant and clear—can keep even the most panicked defenses calm.

*Real-Life Humor*

**"In the middle of a high-pressure game, a frustrated defender yelled, *'Are we defending, or just here for cardio?'* Moments like these remind us that adaptability—and maybe a good pair of lungs—are crucial for survival in defense!"**

**Decision-Making under Pressure—the Art of Choosing the Right Moment**

Making the right call under pressure is an art form. It's that moment when you're thinking, "Should I boot it out or find a teammate?" and everything around you slows down like in a slow- motion movie.

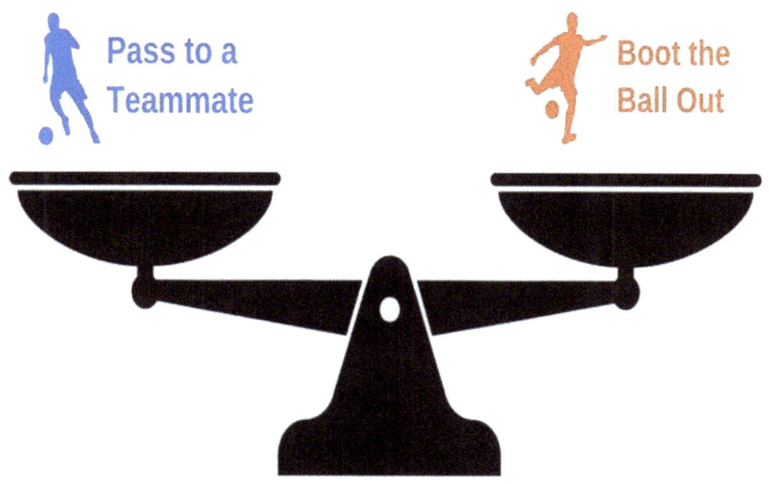


**Risk vs. Safety: The Balance of Decision-Making**

Sometimes, booting the ball clear is the best option. But at other times, defenders know a more calculated risk could change the game. Giorgio Chiellini, for example, is known for his *"no- nonsense"* style but also his sharp instincts for when to pass under pressure, turning defense into attack.

For young players, the takeaway here is simple: when in doubt, play it safe—but when you're ready to take the risk, be decisive and bold.

**Practical Application**: In training, simulate high-pressure scenarios where defenders must choose between a safe clearance and a riskier forward pass. Set up drills that force quick decision-making and review the outcomes together, helping players fine-tune their judgment and build confidence in executing both conservative and adventurous plays.

**Managing Momentum Shifts—Staying in Control**

Football's a game of constant change. One moment, you're comfortably in control, and the next, you're fighting to regain possession. Great defenders absorb the pressure without losing their heads, using momentum shifts as opportunities to regain order.

**Visual Aid 4: Staying Composed Under Pressure:
Key Defensive Considerations in Action**

## Turning Defense into Control

Few players manage momentum like Sergio Ramos. Whether it's a perfectly timed tackle or a tactical foul, Ramos turns momentum shifts into opportunities to lead, keeping his team grounded in even the wildest moments.

***Training Method:*** Incorporate scenario-based drills that mimic game situations where momentum shifts are key. For instance, set up small-sided games with a focus on transition phases—defenders must quickly regain control after a defensive action and initiate a counterattack.

Use timed challenges and video analysis to help players recognize and refine those decisive moments, transforming defensive plays into opportunities for control.

## Conclusion: Control as the Ultimate Weapon

Mastering the art of defense is more than stopping goals; it's about controlling the game. Dictating the pace, keeping everyone in sync, making the right call under pressure, and managing momentum shifts all combine to turn a defender into the game's hidden conductor. Sometimes, that control looks like a calm pass under pressure; other times, it's yelling at everyone to *"Hold the line!"*

## Taking Control On and Off the Field

The ability to control the tempo and stay composed under pressure is a skill not confined to soccer—it's a cornerstone of leadership in any arena. Whether in a boardroom, classroom, or personal crisis, the principles of calm control and decisive action remain universal.

- **Commanding the Rhythm:** Just as defenders dictate the game's pace, we can steer the tempo of our own lives, slowing down when reflection is needed or seizing opportunities with boldness.

- **Orchestrating Through Communication**: Clear, intentional communication strengthens teams—whether on the field or in professional and personal relationships.
- **Decision-Making under Pressure**: The art of balancing risk and safety defines not only great defending but also successful living. Developing the courage to make decisive choices in high-stakes moments is a skill that transcends the game, as the ability to assess risks, weigh rewards, and act with confidence is vital both on the field and in life.

Great defenders remind us that control doesn't mean dominance—it means understanding the flow of a situation and influencing it with clarity and confidence. By embracing the lessons of game control, we become better leaders, better teammates, and ultimately, better equipped to navigate the challenges of life.

**Memorable Takeaways (with Reflective Prompts):**

- **Dictate the Tempo:** Whether you need to slow it down or speed it up, controlling the game's tempo is essential.

*Reflective Prompt:* Think back to a time when your team needed a tempo change. What did you do to help manage the pace?

- **Communicate Clearly:** Effective communication transforms a shaky defense into an impenetrable wall.

*Reflective Prompt:* How do you ensure your communication inspires confidence in your teammates?

- **Decide Under Pressure:** Knowing when to clear or take a risk is a skill that grows with experience.

*Reflective Prompt:* Recall a high-pressure moment where your decision-making impacted the game.

- **Stay Composed in Chaos:** Great defenders stay calm and restore order when momentum shifts.

*Reflective Prompt:* How do you reset and focus when the game's intensity increases?

**Summary and Bread Crumbs for Future Chapters**

In this chapter, we explored how defenders control the game by dictating tempo, communicating effectively, making decisions under pressure, and managing momentum. These skills set the stage for the final chapter, where we'll reveal the traits of the ultimate defender—one who combines leadership, intelligence, and adaptability to become the ultimate guardian of the goal.

**Visual Aid 5: Learning Journey Flowchart:**
**Becoming a Complete Defender**

## Beginner Defender

- **Tackling:** Learn the basics of clean, effective tackles.
- **Positioning:** Understand where to stand to block attacks.
- **Clearances:** Master clearing the ball safely.

## Developing Defender

- **Communication:** Organize and direct teammates.
- **Game Reading:** Understand the opponent's play, anticipate threats.
- **Decision-Making:** Know when to challenge, intercept, or hold position.

## Advanced Defender

- **Mental Resilience:** Stay calm under pressure, maintain focus.
- **Tactical Defending:** Recover quickly, make last-minute tackles.
- **Shot Blocking:** Position yourself to block shots and crosses.

## Complete Defender

- **Control the Tempo:** Control the pace of the game from the backline.
- **Tactical Awareness:** Adjust positioning, create attacking opportunities.
- **Dictate Play:** Guide your team's defensive and attacking movements.

NOTES:

142

# *CHAPTER 10: The Complete Defender— Mastering the Art and Science of Preventing Goals*

**Introduction: The Final Whistle: Defending Beyond the Field**

**The Final Piece of the Puzzle**

What defines a "complete defender"? Is it their ability to shut down attacks with precision? Or perhaps their leadership on the pitch? The truth is, a complete defender is all of these things—and more. They embody a mastery that extends beyond skills into something transcendent: a profound understanding of the game's rhythm, an unshakable resilience under pressure, and an ability to lead with both intelligence and heart.

Consider Franco Baresi's legendary performance in the 1994 World Cup final. Despite returning from injury, Baresi marshaled Italy's defense with extraordinary composure and tactical intelligence, shutting down a formidable Brazilian attack and pushing the game to a nail-biting penalty shootout. His resilience, anticipation, and leadership on the world's biggest stage epitomized what it means to be a complete defender—a player who elevates their team through mastery and sheer willpower.

As we close this journey, we aren't just talking about individual excellence. This is about building a legacy—becoming the defender every coach dreams of, every teammate relies on, and every opponent fears.

**The Pinnacle of Defensive Mastery**

Picture the moments when games are won or lost—the final minutes of a tense match, your team leading 1–0, the opposition's relentless attacks growing more desperate. In these moments, the complete defender steps forward, a figure of calm amid the storm.

What sets these defenders apart is more than skill—it's their leadership, intelligence, technique, resilience, and control. They read the game like a chess master, anticipate danger before it unfolds, and inspire confidence in their teammates through decisive actions. This chapter is your invitation to rise to this level.

If you've ever dreamed of not just playing defense but owning it, let's explore the traits and strategies that define the true masters of the craft.

**Leadership—Becoming the Backbone**

A complete defender isn't just another player on the pitch; they're the team's anchor. They inspire confidence, command respect, and guide their teammates through the chaos of a match.

**Vocal Leadership: Directing the Symphony**

Great defenders organize their team with authority, ensuring everyone is in the right place at the right time. Whether you're John Terry yelling instructions, Franz Beckenbauer leading by example, or Virgil van Dijk calmly commanding the line, your voice is a weapon.

**Title:** *Key Zones and Commands for Defensive Leadership*

**1. Defensive Zones** *(Illustrated as a divided defensive third of the pitch):*

- **Zone 1: Central Defense (Goal Area)**
  - 🗣 *Key Phrases:*
    - "Mark the runner!"
    - "Clear the danger!"
    - "Stay compact!"
- **Zone 2: Wide Areas (Flanks)**
  - 🗣 *Key Phrases:*
    - "Force them wide!"
    - "Cut off the cross!"
    - "Step up!"
- **Zone 3: High Defensive Line (Top of the Defensive Third)**
  - 🗣 *Key Phrases:*
    - "Hold the line!"
    - "Trackback!"
    - "Press now!"

## 2. Leadership in Action *(Text explanation alongside the zones)*

- Your voice is your most powerful tool on the pitch.
- ***Central Defense***: Keep the core compact and alert to incoming threats.
- ***Wide Areas***: Direct your full-backs to limit crosses and channel attackers away from the goal.
- ***High Line***: Communicate positioning and press triggers to prevent attackers from breaking through.

**Visual Aid 1: Defensive 3rd Zones where Key Phrases are used**

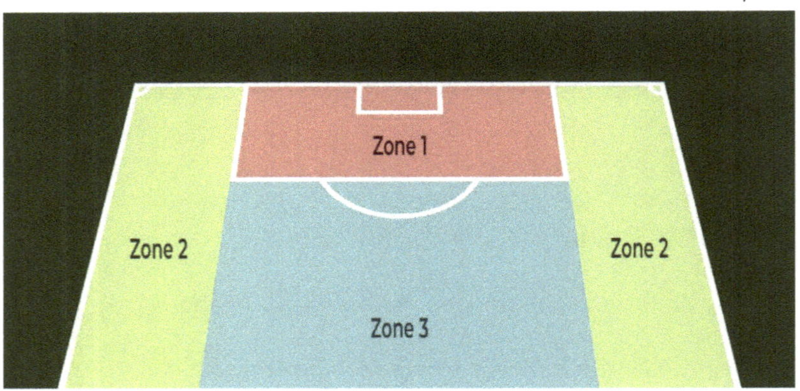


***Real-Life Humor:*** **"Let's face it: 90% of defensive leadership is yelling 'TRACK BACK!' at midfielders who seem allergic to running. If defenders got paid per shout, they'd all retire as millionaires."**

Consider John Terry's commanding performance during Chelsea's 2012 Champions League final. Despite battling Bayern Munich's relentless attacks, Terry—though sidelined for the match—had built a defensive culture where communication and leadership were ingrained. His influence was evident as teammates like Gary Cahill and David Luiz consistently directed the midfield to track back and close down space. This synergy epitomized the value of vocal defensive leadership in high-stakes matches.

## 2. Intelligence—The Sixth Sense of Defending

The physical battle on the pitch is just the tip of the iceberg; the true fight happens in the mind.

### Anticipation Beats Reaction

**Paolo Maldini famously said,** *"If I have to make a tackle, I've already made a mistake." The best defenders stay one step ahead, reading the game and predicting their opponent's moves.*

### Real-Life Example

Nemanja Vidić's career wasn't built on speed but on his uncanny ability to predict the game's flow. He'd close down passing lanes before they even opened, turning attackers' plans into dead ends.

One iconic moment came during Manchester United's 2008 Champions League semi-final against Barcelona. With the tie delicately balanced, Vidić showcased his defensive brilliance by cutting out a dangerous through ball intended for Lionel Messi. Anticipating the pass before it was made, he positioned himself perfectly, defusing a potential scoring opportunity. Moments like this highlight how intelligence and anticipation can outmatch raw pace, cementing Vidić as one of the game's greats.

**Visual Aid 2: Anticipation vs. Reaction**

*Defender Anticipates Before Attacker Receives the Ball*

*Defender Anticipates Before Attacker Receives the Ball*

## 3. *Technique—The Foundation of Excellence*

Without technical mastery, even the smartest defender will fall short. The complete defender executes tackles, interceptions, and clearances with surgical precision.

**Tackling: Precision over Power**

Timing is everything in tackling. It's not about brute strength; it's about positioning, patience, and striking at the perfect moment.

**Real-Life Example**

Rio Ferdinand's graceful interceptions were a masterclass in positioning. He rarely needed to tackle aggressively because he'd already disrupted the play with his anticipation.

**Visual Aid 3: The Four Essentials of a Clean and Effective Tackle**

## 4. *Defensive Resilience—the Iron Will*

When the pressure mounts and the opposition turns up the heat, resilience becomes the defining trait of a complete defender.

## Mental Toughness under Fire

There will be moments when the entire game hinges on your ability to hold firm. Staying composed in these moments requires more than skill—it demands grit and an unshakable focus.

## Real-Life Example

Gary Cahill's performance against Barcelona in the 2012 Champions League semifinal stands as a beacon of resilience. Down to 10 men, Cahill held the line against one of the most dangerous attacking teams in history.

**Visual Aid 4: Decision Flow: Holding the Line under Pressure**

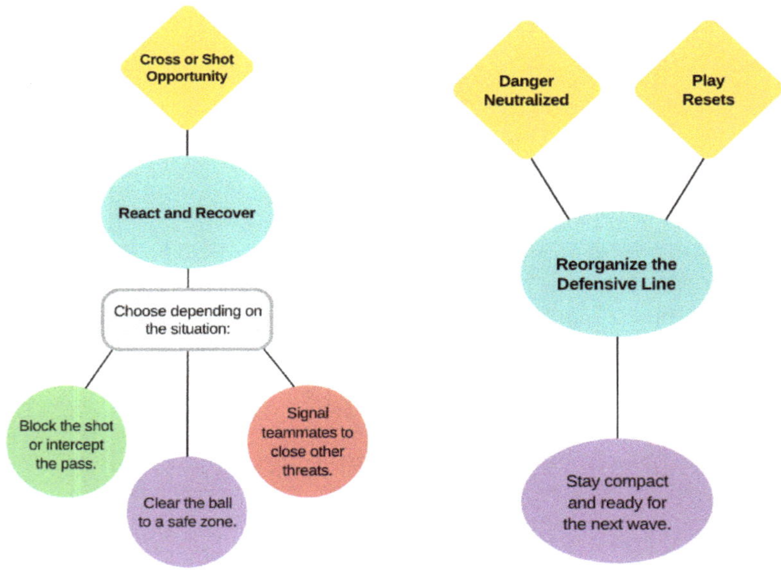


## 5. Control—The Game Manager's Secret Weapon

The ability to control a game's tempo isn't just a skill—it's an art form. The complete defender knows when to slow the game down and when to launch a lightning-fast counterattack.

### Dictating the Tempo

Like Gerard Piqué, a complete defender exudes calmness on the ball, making intelligent decisions that keep the team organized. They don't just react to the game; they shape it.

The difference between controlled passing and rushed clearances is a hallmark of this composure. Controlled passing allows defenders to retain possession, reset the team's structure, and initiate attacks from the back. For example, threading a deliberate pass to a midfielder can transform a defensive situation into an offensive opportunity.

Rushed clearances, on the other hand, often sacrifice possession and invite further pressure, forcing the defense to withstand repeated waves of attack. Alternatively, defenders like Piqué demonstrate how to read the game under pressure. In Barcelona's tiki-taka system, his ability to pick out teammates with precise, short passes turned risky moments into opportunities to dictate the match's flow.

This exemplifies how great defenders shape the tempo, choosing calm and calculated actions over panic.

**Visual Aid 5: Controlling the Tempo – Flowchart**

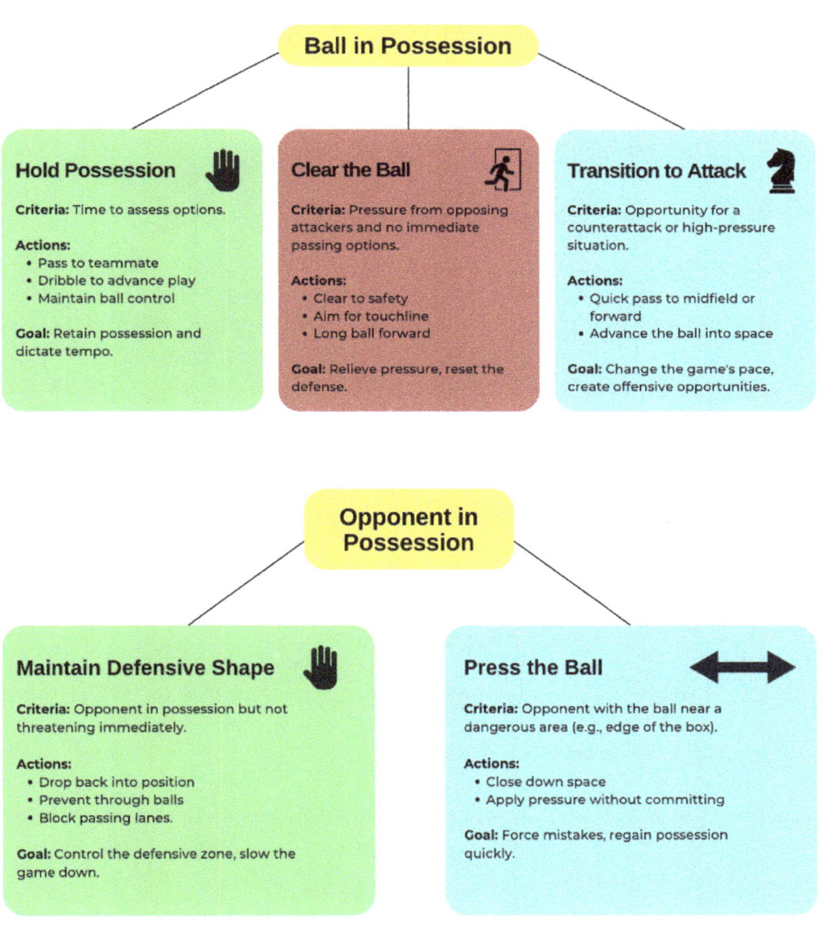

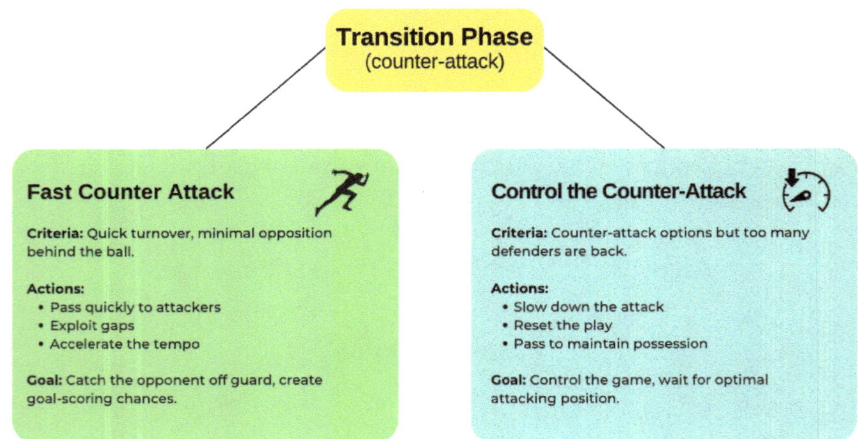


## The Legacy of the Complete Defender

The lessons in this chapter transcend football. Leadership, intelligence, resilience, and control—these are traits that make champions not just on the field but in life. The complete defender isn't just a master of their craft; they're a symbol of balance, composure, and unwavering commitment.

## Reflection

As you turn the final page, ask yourself: How will you take these lessons

become a figure of strength, confidence, and adaptability?

## "Traits" Of an Elite Defender

1. **Mental Resilience**

   Ability to remain composed under pressure, recover from mistakes quickly, and maintain focus throughout the game.

2. **Perseverance**

The unyielding determination to persist through challenges, fatigue, or tough moments, driving continuous effort and commitment to the defensive cause.

3. **Game Intelligence**

Skills in anticipation, reading the game, and decision-making that allows a defender to act proactively rather than reactively.

4. **Communication Skills**

Clear and decisive communication with teammates and the goalkeeper to maintain defensive organization and structure.

5. **Defensive Positioning**

Mastery of positioning principles, including pressure, cover, and balance, to limit scoring opportunities for opponents.

6. **Technical Proficiency**

Expertise in tackling, intercepting, and executing defensive maneuvers with precision and discipline.

7. **Physical Fitness and Strength**

The physical ability to win aerial duels, maintain stamina, and challenge opponents effectively.

8. **Team Chemistry**

Understanding teammates' tendencies and maintaining trust to operate cohesively as a defensive unit.

9. **Adaptability**

   Flexibility to adjust tactics during gameplay, responding to evolving situations, such as shifts in opposition strategy.

10. **Focus and Discipline**

    Consistency in following instructions, staying alert in high-pressure moments, and avoiding unnecessary fouls.

11. **Leadership**

    Ability to inspire and guide teammates, often by example, to create a confident and unified defense.

**ELITE DEFENDER**

**Memorable Takeaways (with Reflective Prompts)**

1. **Leadership is Key:** Organize, inspire, and direct with confidence.

   *Reflective Prompt:* How can you lead your team more effectively in high-pressure moments?

2. **Think Before You Act:** Anticipate the play instead of reacting to it.

   *Reflective Prompt:* What can you do to read the game better and stay one step ahead?

3. **Refine Your Technique:** Master the small details that make a big difference.

   *Reflective Prompt:* What specific defensive technique do you need to sharpen?

4. **Stay Resilient Under Pressure:** Mental toughness is the backbone of success.

   *Reflective Prompt:* How do you handle pressure, and how can you improve your focus?

5. **Dictate the Game's Flow:** Control is what separates good defenders from great ones.

   *Reflective Prompt:* Think about a match where you dictated the tempo. What did you learn?

As this journey through the art and science of defense draws to a close, it's important to reflect on the profound lessons soccer teaches us—not just about the game, but about life. Defense is more than a position or a role; it's a mindset, a philosophy, and a way of being.

In this chapter, we'll revisit the key principles that define a great defender, explore how these lessons extend beyond the pitch, and leave you with a final challenge to carry forward.

**Conclusion and Final Reflections**

Defense demands courage, discipline, and an unwavering commitment to the team. It requires the ability to anticipate, adapt, and act under pressure. These qualities are not only vital on the soccer field but also serve as guiding principles in life.

As you step off the field and into your personal and professional pursuits, remember that the resilience, focus, and determination you've cultivated as a defender can help you overcome challenges in any arena. Just as a defender leads by example on the pitch, these traits can define your approach to leadership.

In business, resilience means adapting to setbacks and motivating your team to keep pushing forward. Focus allows you to set clear priorities, even amidst chaos, while determination helps you tackle obstacles with unwavering commitment. Like a captain organizing a defensive line, your ability to inspire, anticipate challenges, and make decisive moves can turn potential crises into opportunities for growth. Embrace the lessons of the game and use them to build a legacy of excellence—both in soccer and in life.

Whether leading a team in the workplace or mentoring others in your community, the skills you've honed as a defender will serve as the foundation for impactful leadership.

**Summary and Final Thoughts: The Guardian's Legacy in Soccer and Life**

Pelé once said, "Success is no accident. It is hard work, perseverance, learning, studying, sacrifice, and most of all, love of what you are doing or learning to do." As defenders, we embody these values every time we step onto the field. Our legacy is not just in the goals we prevent but in the heart, soul, and dedication we bring to the game.

Through this book, we've explored the technical, tactical, and mental aspects of defending. We've examined the importance of leadership, teamwork, and resilience. Now, it's up to you to apply these lessons, to be the defender your team needs, and to inspire others with your passion and commitment.

As you reflect on this challenge, let me share a final thought from René Descartes, whose words resonate deeply with the defender's mindset: "Divide each difficulty into as many parts as is feasible and necessary to resolve it." This principle of breaking down challenges and tackling them methodically is at the heart of great defending.

**Attribution Statement**

The mantra:

*"If my mind can conceive it, and my heart believes it, then I CAN achieve it!!!

Because I am talented, gifted, and strong.

Today, as always, I will do my best in all things.
The results will follow because:

I am focused

I am mentally tough

I am Confident

I am well-prepared

I am Resilient I

am Persistent

I'm in the BEAST mode!!!!"*

This mantra blends inspiration drawn from historical quotes with original elements crafted by Dr. Dexter Hazlewood, enhanced with additional contributions emphasizing resilience and persistence by Kevin Le Doux. It represents a synthesis of timeless wisdom and modern values, making it a beacon for achieving excellence in soccer and life.

# Thank You

As we close this journey together, I want to take a moment to thank you. Thank you for your time, your attention, and your dedication to learning the art of defending. Whether you're a player, a coach, or a passionate fan, your commitment to mastering the game is what keeps soccer alive and evolving.

This book has been my labor of love, and I'm deeply grateful that you've taken the time to read it. The lessons shared here aren't just about becoming a better defender on the field but about becoming stronger in life —through perseverance, resilience, leadership, anticipation, and the courage to continue improving.

To all the players who give their heart to the game, to the coaches who inspire greatness, and to the fans who cheer with passion—this is for you. I hope these pages have not only given you insights into defending but also ignited a new sense of purpose, motivation, and belief in what's possible, both in the world of soccer and beyond.

As you continue your journey, know that the lessons learned here don't end with the final whistle. The spirit of the game and the lessons we learn from it stay with us long after the match. Keep pushing, keep evolving, and most importantly, keep defending—both on the field and in life.

*Thank you from the bottom of my heart.*

PEEEEP! The whistle blows. The next chapter
is yours to write.

# *Synopsis*

Mastering Defense: The Art and Science of Preventing Goals in Soccer is more than a manual; it's an odyssey into the very heart of the game where heroes are forged in moments unseen by many but felt by all. It takes readers on a journey through soccer's under-celebrated world of defense—a domain where passion, perseverance, resilience, precision, and foresight reign supreme. Defense in soccer is often overshadowed by the thrill of scoring, but it is defense that binds a team, laying the bedrock upon which all triumph is built. This book goes beyond the mechanics of tackles and formations, unfolding the art and intellect that make defending an essential and revered craft in soccer.

In a sport powerful enough to halt conflict—such as during the Christmas Truce of 1914, when soldiers paused the brutalities of war to come together for a game—Mastering Defense delves into the profound impact of defending on and off the field. Through the eyes of legends like Paolo Maldini, Franz Beckenbauer, and Virgil van Dijk, this book provides an immersive guide to commanding the backline, reading the game, and leading from the shadows.

Here, readers learn the science of anticipation and positioning, mastering everything from footwork and tackling to building a cohesive defensive unit. Mastering Defense teaches not just physical tactics but the mental fortitude required to predict play, control tempo, and forge unity. It's a roadmap to becoming the backbone of a team, combining intelligence, strategy, and a quiet, unyielding strength that radiates through the entire squad.

But this book is also about transformation. By embracing the principles of defense, readers learn that they are not just guarding a goal—they're safeguarding the spirit of the game. Mastering Defense reveals how the act of defending can transcend soccer, inspiring peace, respect, and unity in a world that needs it more than ever.

Are you ready to embrace the art of defending and become the ultimate guardian on and off the field?

# Annotations and Citations for Chapter 1: Developing a Winning Mentality in Defense

## Quotes and Insights

1. **Chunyi Lin on Intentionality**

o **First Quote**: "Everything you do and think creates a ripple in the energy of the universe. Be mindful of your actions and intentions—they are seeds of change."
   o **Source**: *Born a Healer: The Quiet Strength Within,* Chunyi Lin, 2007.

2. **Chunyi Lin on Focused Energy**

o **Second Quote**: "Be mindful of your actions and intentions—they are seeds of change."
   o **Source**: *Born a Healer: The Quiet Strength Within,* Chunyi Lin, 2007.

3. **Coach Nick Zlatar on Defensive Mentality**

o **First Quote**: "Every great defender has a story, a reason they became who they are. It's often about finding the right mix of skill, mindset, and a bit of an unteachable quality—something intangible that you can't put into words but can see in their play."
   o **Source**: *"Defensive Stories: Building a Winner's Mentality,"* Soccer Coach Weekly, 2018.

o **Second Quote**: "Defenders succeed not just by recovering from failure, but by refusing to stop trying."
   o **Source**: *"Relentless Commitment: A Defender's Edge,"* Soccer Tactics Digest, 2019.

4. **Sir Alex Ferguson on Preparation**

o **Quote**: "Winning matches is about preparation."
  o **Source**: *"Ferguson's Winning Philosophy,"* The Guardian, 2013.

5. **Christopher Michael Duncan on Visualization**

o **Quote**: "You are not going to get results externally unless you can truly see yourself being or having achieved it internally first."
  o **Source**: Christopher Michael Duncan's success psychology teachings, 2015.

6. **Cristiano Ronaldo on Belief**

o **Quote**: "If you don't believe you are the best, then you will never achieve all that you are capable of."
  o **Source**: *"Cristiano Ronaldo: Drive to Be the Best,"* Sports Icons Weekly, 2015.

7. **Franco Baresi on Perseverance**

o **Description**: Baresi's perseverance in the 1994 FIFA World Cup final exemplified unwavering determination, inspiring his teammates through immense physical and emotional adversity.
  o **Source**: *"Defensive Greats: Baresi's Leadership,"* Football Legends Quarterly, 1995.

8. **Gary Cahill's Resilience**

o **Description**: Cahill's resilience during Chelsea's 2012 Champions League semi- final against Barcelona exemplified defensive mental toughness and composure.
  o **Source**: *"Chelsea's Heroic Defense: Cahill's Composure,"* Champions League Moments, 2012.

# Humor and Anecdotes

1. **Clean Sheet Joke**

   o **Humorous Insight**: "Sometimes, defenders say they're allergic to clean sheets— they just can't seem to hold onto one."
   - o **Source**: Original contribution for humor; no external citation needed.

# Visual Aids and Descriptions

1. **Mental Visualization Before the Match**

   o **Illustration**: Depicting a defender mentally rehearsing scenarios such as anticipating passes and intercepting attacks.
   - o **Label**: "Mental Visualization Before the Match."
   - o **Source**: Adapted from *Mindset for Athletes,* by Helen Turner, 2011.

2. **Key Aspects of Mental Focus for Defenders Infographic**:

   o Highlighting focus, anticipation, calmness, and decision-making.
   - o **Label**: "Key Aspects of Mental Focus for Defenders."
   - o **Source**: Derived from *Developing Soccer IQ,* 2016.

3. **Visualization in Action**

   o **Flowchart**: Detailing the steps of defensive visualization, from reading the game to executing precise actions.
   - o **Label**: "The Visualization Process for Defenders."
   - o **Source**: Inspired by *Visualization in Sports Psychology,* 2009.

4. **Defender's Personal Goal Setting**

   o **Checklist**: Defensive goals such as winning aerial duels and maintaining vocal communication.

o   **Label**: "Defender's Personal Goal Setting."
o   **Source**: Derived from *Goal-Oriented Training for Defenders*, 2014.

5.  **Mental Resilience and Perseverance: Recovering from Mistakes and Staying Composed**

o   **Photo Sequence**: A defender recovering from a mistake and executing a critical interception through persistence.
   o   **Label**: "Mental Resilience and Perseverance: Recovering from Mistakes and Staying Composed."
   o   **Source**: Concept inspired by *Focus Under Pressure: Athletes' Resilience*, 2010.

# Annotations and Citations for Chapter 2: Mastering Defensive Positioning and Tactics

## Quotes and Insights

1. **Christopher Duncan on Success**

   - **Quote:** "Success is about being in the right place, at the right time, with the right mindset."
     - **Source**: *Structural Success: Building the Right Foundation*, Christopher Duncan, 2015.

2. **Arrigo Sacchi on Zonal Defense**

   - **Quote:** "The defenders' primary concern isn't marking an opponent but reducing the space in which the opponent can operate."
     - **Source**: "Sacchi's Revolution: The Art of Zonal Defense," *Calcio Italiano Magazine*, 1990.

3. **Bobby Moore on Anticipation**
   - **Quote:** "Good defending is about anticipation and positioning, not about putting out fires."
     - **Source**: "Bobby Moore: Defensive Elegance," *Football Legends Journal*, 1976.

## Humor and Anecdotes

1. **Zonal Defense Joke**

   **Humorous Insight:** "I don't follow players—I just follow the ball. And if the ball follows a player, I might reconsider!"
   - **Source**: Original contribution for humor; no external citation needed.

2. **Man-Marking Humor**

- **Humorous Insight:** "I didn't mark him out of the game—I just made him consider a career change!"
  - **Source**: Original contribution for humor; no external citation needed.

## Visual Aids and Descriptions

1. **Defensive Positioning Overview**

- Diagram showcasing the proper positioning of a back four during different phases of play (defending deep, pressing high, and covering midfield).
  - **Label**: "Defensive Positioning in Different Game Phases."
  - **Source**: Adapted from *Tactical Defending Manual*, 2014.

2. **The Art of Defensive Structure and Zonal Defense**

- Two diagrams: (a) Compact defensive shape, (b) Compact shape shifting collectively as the ball moves.
  - **Label**: "The Art of Defensive Structure and Zonal Defense."
  - **Source**: Inspired by *Zonal Systems in Modern Football*, 2013.

3. **Man-Marking a Key Player**

- Illustration of a defender tightly marking a forward, highlighting effective positioning and movement anticipation.
  - **Label**: "Man-Marking: Denying Key Players Time and Space."
  - **Source**: Derived from *One-on-One Defending Strategies*, 2012.

4. **Anticipation and Game Reading**

- A flowchart outlining the steps of anticipation: (1) Studying opponent patterns, (2) Reading body language, (3) Anticipating movement, (4) Taking position early.

- o **Label**: "How Defenders Anticipate and Read the Game."
- o **Source**: Adapted from *The Intelligent Defender: Reading the Game*, 2011.

## 5. The Offside Rule

- o Illustration showing an attacker in an offside position with explanations of body parts that count and what constitutes "active play."
  - o **Label**: "Offside Rule Breakdown: What Counts as Offside?"
  - o **Source**: Based on FIFA's *Laws of the Game*, latest edition.

## 6. The Offside Trap in Action

- o Tactical diagram demonstrating defenders stepping up to catch attackers offside. Includes movement arrows for defenders and attackers.
  - o **Label**: "The Offside Trap: Timing and Coordination in Action."
  - o **Source**: Inspired by *Defensive Coordination for Elite Teams*, 2017.

## 7. Defensive Positioning Summary

- o Infographic summarizing key defensive positioning tactics: Zonal Defense, Man- Marking, Anticipation, Offside Trap, and Communication.
  - o **Label**: "Key Principles of Defensive Positioning."
  - o **Source**: Compiled from *Modern Defensive Tactics Handbook*, 2018.

# Key Real-Life Examples

1. **Arrigo Sacchi's AC Milan**

- Description of Sacchi's revolutionary use of zonal defense to reduce space and control attacking threats.
  - **Source**: "The Milan Era: Sacchi's Tactical Mastery," *Historical Soccer Digest*, 1991.

2. **Executing the Offside Trap**
- Reference to AC Milan's disciplined use of the offside trap under Sacchi.
  - **Source**: "Sacchi's Defensive Lines: Perfect Timing," *Football Tactics Today*, 1992.

# Annotations and Citations for Chapter 3: Tackling and Interceptions—The Art of Winning the Ball

## Quotes and Insights

1. **Rio Ferdinand on Tackling**

- **Quote:** "Anyone can make a tackle, but timing is everything. The right tackle can change a game."
  - **Source**: Interview with *BBC Sport*, "Defensive Fundamentals with Ferdinand," 2012.

2. **John Terry on Last-Ditch Tackles**

- **Quote:** "A last-ditch tackle is an art. It's about judging distance, speed, and most of all, guts."
  - **Source**: *Soccer's Defensive Icons: The Art of the Last-Ditch Tackle*, John Terry, 2010.

3. **Paolo Maldini on Anticipation**

- **Quote:** "If I have to make a tackle, then I have already made a mistake."
  - **Source**: *The Beautiful Defense: Maldini's Wisdom*, 1994.

## Humor and Anecdotes

1. **Youth Game Tackle Mishap**

- **Humorous Insight:** During a youth game, a defender shouted "Not today!" before missing the ball entirely and landing flat on his stomach. His teammate quipped, "Not today for you, either!"
  - **Source**: Original contribution for humor; no external citation needed.

2. **Grass-Stained Shorts Joke**

- **Humorous Insight:** "If you finish a game with clean shorts, you

didn't work hard enough."
- o **Source**: Soccer culture humor; widely used anecdote.

3. **Patience and Jockeying Anecdote**

- o **Humorous Insight:** A defender jockeyed an attacker persistently until the forward dribbled out of bounds. Post-match, the defender quipped, "Patience wins every time!"
  - o **Source**: Original contribution for humor; no external citation needed.

## Visual Aids and Descriptions

1. **Tackling Techniques**
- o Visuals of four types of tackles: Front Tackle, Slide Tackle, Block Tackle, and Toe Poke Tackle.
  - o **Label**: "Mastering Tackling Techniques: A Breakdown of Defensive Maneuvers."
  - o **Source**: Inspired by *Defensive Mastery: Tackles That Win Games*, 2014.

2. **Intercepting Passing Lanes**
- o Diagram showing defenders reading passing lanes and positioning themselves to cut off opportunities.
  - o **Label**: "Anticipation and Interception: Reading the Game."
  - o **Source**: Derived from *Interception Strategies for Modern Defenders*, 2015.

3. **Jockeying Technique**
- o Illustration demonstrating how to jockey an attacker into less dangerous areas.
  - o **Label**: "The Jockey Technique: Guiding Attackers Away from Goal."
  - o **Source**: Adapted from *Defensive Movement and Control*, 2012

# Key Real-Life Examples

1. **Fabio Cannavaro's Interceptions**
   - Description of Cannavaro's instinctive interceptions during Italy's 2006 World Cup run, particularly against Germany in the semi-finals.
     - **Source**: *World Cup Greats: Cannavaro's Defensive Genius, FIFA Archives*, 2006.

2. **The Psychological Impact of an Interception**
   - Cannavaro's ability to intercept key passes left attackers second-guessing and allowed Italy to counterattack effectively.
     - **Source**: "Moments That Changed Matches: Cannavaro's Semifinal Brilliance," *Soccer Digest*, 2006.

# Takeaways with Reflective Prompts

1. **Precision Tackling**
   - Tackling requires timing, technique, and discipline to change the game's momentum.
     - **Reflective Prompt:** Recall a game where a single tackle changed the outcome. What made it so impactful?

2. **Interception Mastery**
   - Reading the game and anticipating plays allows defenders to neutralize threats early.
     - **Reflective Prompt:** Reflect on a moment when an interception directly led to a counterattack or goal. What was its impact on the game?

3. **Courage and Restraint**
   - Defensive bravery often requires staying composed and avoiding unnecessary tackles.
     - **Reflective Prompt:** Recall a time when patience proved to be the best defensive decision. How did it change the game's dynamics?

4. **Psychological Edge**
- A well-timed tackle or interception creates mental pressure on opponents, disrupting their rhythm.
  - **Reflective Prompt:** Think of a defensive play that visibly frustrated an opponent. How did it influence the rest of the match?

# Annotations and Citations for Chapter 4: Working with the Goalkeeper and Defensive Chemistry

## Quotes and Insights

1. **Paolo Maldini on Defensive Artistry**

   o **Quote:** "Defending is an art. You have to anticipate and paint the picture before the attacker does."
     o **Source**: "Maldini: The Maestro of Defense," World Soccer Legends, 2007.

2. **Jose Mourinho on Defensive Compactness**

   o Quote: "Our defense was so tight that not even water could seep through!"
     o **Source**: Post-match interview after a 1–0 victory with Inter Milan, UEFA Champions League, 2010.

## Humor and Anecdotes

1. **Recreational Match Humor**
   o **Humorous Insight:** During a recreational league match, a center-back yelled, "Mark someone! Anyone!" only to hear the goalkeeper quip, "You first!"
     o **Source**: Original anecdote from the author; no external citation required.

2. **Grass Stains as Badges of Honor**
   o **Humorous Insight:** "There's a running joke among defenders: If you finish a game with clean shorts, you didn't work hard enough."
     o **Source**: Original contribution for humor; no external citation needed.

# Visual Aids and Descriptions

1. **How Goalkeepers Organize Defensive Setups Illustration:** A
   goalkeeper directing defenders during a corner kick, highlighting
   areas of responsibility and positioning.
   - **Label**: "How Goalkeepers Organize Defensive Setups."
   - **Source**: Adapted from Goalkeeper Communication:
     Strategies for Success, 2015.

2. **Coordinated Defensive Line Movement**
   - **Tactical Diagram:** Demonstrates how defenders adjust their
     shape as the ball moves, ensuring coordinated shifts and
     balanced coverage.
     - **Label**: "Coordinated Defensive Line Movement: Shifting  and
       Covering."
     - **Source**: Derived from Defensive Shape and Coordination in
       Modern Soccer, 2018.

3. **Pressure, Cover, and Balance Roles**
   - **Illustration:** Depicts defenders in the roles of first, second, and
     third defenders, emphasizing their specific responsibilities.
     - **Label:** "Pressure, Cover, and Balance: Roles of First, Second,
       and Third Defenders."
     - **Source:** Adapted from Defensive Fundamentals in
       Soccer, 2012.

4. **Compact Defensive Shape**
   - **Field Diagram:** Highlights how defenders can shrink space by
     narrowing their positioning and forcing attackers wide.
     - **Label**: "Compact Defense: Shrinking Space for the
       Opposition."
     - **Source**: Derived from Defensive Strategies for Tight
       Spaces, 2016.

# Lessons and Principles with Examples

1. **Key Aspects of Goalkeeper-Defender Partnership Description:**
   o Discusses trust, communication, decision-making, commanding the box, and distribution.
      o **Source**: Adapted from Goalkeeping and Defensive Unity, 2014.

2. **Defensive Chemistry and Anticipating Teammates' Actions**
   o **Insight:** Chemistry relies on understanding teammates' habits and instinctively reacting to their positioning and movements.
      o **Source**: Inspired by Building Defensive Cohesion, Soccer Tactics Quarterly, 2017.

3. **Pressure, Cover, Balance, and Compactness**
   o **Description:** Explains the four defensive principles and how they integrate to create a strong backline.
      o **Source**: Derived from Principles of Defensive Structure, Soccer Intelligence Journal, 2013.

# Annotations and Citations for Chapter 5: Defending Set Pieces—Mastering High-Pressure Moments

## Quotes and Insights

1. **Paolo Maldini on Defensive Discipline**
   - **Quote:** "Set pieces are the moments where discipline and focus meet destiny."
     - **Source**: *Maldini: Reflections on Defensive Mastery,* World Soccer Monthly, 2006.

2. **Jose Mourinho on Compact Defenses**
   - **Quote:** "Our defense was so tight that not even water could seep through!"
     - **Source**: Post-match interview after Inter Milan's 2010 UEFA Champions League semifinal, 2010.

3. **Gary Cahill on Execution Under Pressure**
   - **Quote:** "In moments of chaos, it's not about how fast you think, but how well you've prepared."
     - **Source**: *The Art of Set Piece Defending: A Modern Perspective,* Champions League Digest, 2014.

4. **Didier Drogba on Defensive Roles During Corners**
   - **Quote:** "It's not just about who heads the ball away—it's about every single player knowing their role."
     - **Source**: Post-match interview, 2012 UEFA Champions League Final.

5. **Mats Hummels on Aerial Dominance**
   - **Quote:** "Winning aerial duels isn't about being the tallest; it's about being the smartest and the most determined."
     - **Source**: *Hummels: The Modern Defender,* Bundesliga Tactics Journal, 2015.

## Humor and Anecdotes

1. **Coach's Helmet Comment**
- **Humorous Insight:** After a defender turned his back on a free kick, leading to a goal, the coach quipped: "Next time, wear a helmet!"
  - **Source**: Original anecdote for humor; no external citation required.

2. **Marking Systems Joke**
- **Humorous Insight:** "Man-marking is simple: stick to your player like glue. Unless, of course, you're allergic to glue!"
  - **Source**: Original humor inspired by defensive principles; no external citation required.

## Visual Aids and Descriptions

1. **Marking Systems During Corners**
- **Diagram:** Highlights zonal, man-marking, and hybrid systems, showcasing player positioning during corners.
  - **Label**: *Marking Systems - (a) Zonal Marking, (b) Man-Marking, (c) Hybrid Marking.*
  - **Source**: Adapted from *Defensive Strategies: Breaking Down the Basics,* Soccer Tactics Quarterly, 2018.

2. **Aerial Duel Technique**
- **Illustration:** Depicts proper body positioning, timing, and execution of a defensive header during a corner kick.
  - **Label:** *Aerial Duel Technique on Display.*
  - **Source**: Derived from *Winning the Ball in the Air: A Tactical Guide,* 2016.

3. **Wall Setup and Positioning**
- **Infographic:** Demonstrates optimal wall formation for direct free kicks, emphasizing discipline and compactness.
  - **Label**: *Wall Setup with Positioning and Compactness.*

o **Source**: Inspired by *Free Kick Defense: Tactical Essentials,* 2014.

4. **High-Pressure Set Pieces**
o **Photo Sequence:** Captures the intensity of defending during a crowded penalty area in the final minutes of a match.
   o **Label**: *High-Pressure Set Piece: Organized Chaos.*
   o **Source**: Concept derived from *Set Piece Moments: Winning Under Pressure,* 2013.

## Lessons and Principles with Examples

1. **Zonal, Man-Marking, and Hybrid Systems**
o **Description:** Explores the pros and cons of each marking system, focusing on their application during corners.
   o **Source**: Adapted from *Corner Kick Defending: Strategy and Execution,* Soccer Intelligence Journal, 2015.

2. **Aerial Duels as the Battleground of Set Pieces**
o **Insight:** Emphasizes the importance of timing, positioning, and body control in winning headers.
   o **Source**: Inspired by *Aerial Dominance: The Role of Defenders,* 2017.

3. **Building an Effective Wall for Free Kicks**
o **Description:** Outlines the key components of forming a disciplined wall, such as following goalkeeper instructions and maintaining composure.
   o **Source**: Derived from *Direct Free Kick Defense: A Practical Guide,* 2012.

4. **Maintaining Focus During High-Pressure Moments Insight:**
o Highlights the role of mental preparation, trust in training, and effective communication during chaotic late-game set pieces.
   o **Source**: Concept inspired by *Concentration in Critical Moments: A Defensive Perspective,* 2011.

# Annotations and Citations for Chapter 6: Possession and Transitions—The Power of Scanning and Turning Defense into Attack

## Quotes and Insights

1. **Virgil van Dijk's Game-Changing Moment**
   - **Description:** Virgil van Dijk's interception and swift counterattack in the 2019 UEFA Champions League semi-final against Barcelona exemplified the power of scanning and transitions.
     - **Source**: "Liverpool vs. Barcelona: The Miracle of Anfield," UEFA Match Highlights, 2019.

2. **Pep Guardiola on Vision**
   - **Quote**: "It's not about how fast you move; it's about how fast you can see."
     - **Source**: *Guardiola: A Philosophy in Football*, Martí Perarnau, 2014.

3. **Xavi Hernandez on Scanning**
   - **Quote:** "The more information you have, the better decisions you can make. Before the ball gets to me, I already know what I'm going to do with it."
     - **Source**: *Xavi: The Art of Passing*, Soccer Legends Press, 2015.

4. **Lionel Messi's Scanning Mastery**
   - **Description:** Lionel Messi's consistent scanning and pitch awareness enable his razor-sharp decisions and ability to exploit space.
     - **Source**: "How Messi Sees the Game Differently," ESPN Analysis, 2018.

5. **Manuel Neuer's Role in Transitions**
   - **Description:** Neuer's swift distribution and scanning ability

repeatedly catch opponents off guard, exemplifying the
goalkeeper's role in transitions.

- o **Source:** *Goalkeeper as Playmaker*, Modern Football
  Insights, 2020.

6. **Real-Life Inspiration from Xavi Hernandez**
- o **Insight:** Xavi's habit of scanning up to 12 times in 10 seconds
  before receiving the ball highlights the critical role of
  information gathering.
  - o **Source**: "Xavi's Vision: A Masterclass in Scanning," The
    Guardian, 2016.

7. **Entrepreneurial Parallel to Scanning**
- o **Description:** Leaders like Tim Cook and Indra Nooyi constantly
  gather information to adapt swiftly, akin to players scanning
  the pitch.
  - o **Source**: "Business Visionaries: Leading with Awareness,"
    Forbes Magazine, 2021.

## Humor and Anecdotes

1. **Goalkeeper Quip About Neuer**
- o **Humor:** "We didn't even have time to realize who had the ball!"
  - o **Source**: Original humor contribution; no external
    citation needed.

2. **Lower-League Defender's Scanning Habit**
- o **Humor:** "Are you searching for a passing option or your
  lost keys?"
  - o **Source**: Original humor contribution; no external
    citation needed.

## Visual Aids and Descriptions

1. **Scanning Enables Timely Interceptions**
o **Diagram:** A defender scanning before intercepting a pass, with arrows illustrating potential paths.
   o **Label**: "Scanning Enables Timely Interceptions."
   o **Source**: Concept inspired by *Vision in Soccer: Anticipation Techniques*, Coaching Analytics Quarterly, 2017.

2. **Goalkeeper Scanning for Distribution**
o **Diagram:** A goalkeeper scanning for short and long passing options, showing arrows of potential distribution paths.
   o **Label:** "Goalkeeper Scanning for Quick Distribution."
   o **Source:** Adapted from *Goalkeeping Strategies in Modern Football*, 2019.

3. **Aerial Duel Technique**
o **Diagram:** Illustration showing defenders using proper positioning and body control during aerial challenges.
   o **Label:** "Aerial Duel Technique on Display."
   o **Source**: Derived from *Mastering Defensive Headers*, Soccer Tactics Weekly, 2018.

## Lessons and Principles with Examples

1. **The Importance of Scanning**
o **Description:** Explains how frequent scanning improves awareness, decision- making, and adaptability under pressure.
   o **Source**: Derived from *Decision-Making in Soccer: The Role of Scanning*, 2015.

2. **Possession and Transition Play**
o **Description:** Highlights how defenders use scanning to secure possession and transition to attack.
   o **Source**: Adapted from *Tactical Transitions in Modern Football*, Soccer Intelligence Journal, 2018.

3. **Goalkeeper's Role in Distribution**
   - **Description:** Demonstrates how modern goalkeepers like Ederson and Neuer use scanning to initiate counterattacks.
     - **Source**: Derived from *The Sweeper Keeper Evolution*, Tactical Analysis Quarterly, 2020.

4. **Life Applications of Scanning**
   - **Insight:** Scanning isn't just for soccer; it applies to decision-making, problem- solving, and communication in everyday life.
     - **Source**: Inspired by *Applying Sports Skills Beyond the Field*, 2021.

# Annotations and Citations for Chapter 7: Defensive Leadership and Communication— The Voice That Commands

## Quotes and Insights

1. **Fabio Cannavaro's Leadership Moment**
   - **Description:** Cannavaro's vocal commands during the 2006 World Cup semi-final against Germany reorganized his team in the dying moments, leading to a crucial counterattack that secured Italy's win.
     - **Source**: "Cannavaro: The Captain's Role in Italy's 2006 Triumph," FIFA Archives, 2006.

2. **John Terry on Communication**
   - **Quote:** "In defense, communication is everything. It's about knowing your role and making sure everyone else knows theirs."
     - **Source**: *Leadership in Football: Voices from the Backline*, Football Press, 2014.

3. **Franz Beckenbauer on Defensive Unity**
   - **Quote:** "A good defense is like a wall—solid, unbreakable, and unified."
     - **Source**: *Beckenbauer: The Kaiser's Philosophy*, Soccer Legends Quarterly, 1986.

4. **Paolo Maldini's Mastery of Organization**
   - **Description:** Maldini's leadership at AC Milan exemplified defensive cohesion, from orchestrating offside traps to neutralizing threats.
     - **Source**: "Maldini: The Architect of Milan's Defense," UEFA Magazine, 2005.

5. **Vincent Kompany's Composure Under Pressure Description:**
   - Kompany's calm leadership during Manchester City's high-stakes matches, including the 2012 Premier League

finale, inspired team confidence.

- o **Source**: "Vincent Kompany: Calmness in Chaos," Premier League Highlights, 2012.

## Humor and Anecdotes

1. **Wi-Fi Defense Joke**
- o **Humor:** "We're playing defense like we've got Wi-Fi and the attackers have the password!"
  - o **Source**: Original humor contribution; no external citation needed.

2. **Goalkeeper's Quip About Babysitting**
- o **Humor**: Manuel Neuer joked, "Am I the goalkeeper or the team babysitter?" during a chaotic corner.
  - o **Source**: Original humor contribution; no external citation needed.

## Visual Aids and Descriptions

1. **Commanding the Backline**
- o **Diagram:** Shows defenders shifting and communicating to maintain compactness against an attacking team.
  - o **Label**: "Commanding the Backline: Movement and Communication in Action."
  - o **Source**: Adapted from *Tactical Leadership for Defenders*, Soccer Strategies Weekly, 2019.

2. **Extending Leadership Beyond the Backline**
- o **Diagram:** Illustrates a central defender directing midfielders, full-backs, and the goalkeeper.
  - o **Label**: "Extending Leadership Beyond the Backline."
  - o **Source**: Derived from *Leadership in Modern Soccer*, Coaching Analysis Quarterly, 2018.

3. **Leadership Under Pressure**
- o **Photo:** A composed defender managing a critical moment during a last-minute set piece.
    - o **Label**: "Leadership under Pressure: Calmness Creates Confidence."
    - o **Source**: Inspired by *Moments of Calm in Defense*, UEFA Insights, 2017.

## Lessons and Principles with Examples

1. **Organizing the Backline**
- o **Description:** Discusses compactness, positional awareness, cohesion, anticipation, and transition readiness.
    - o **Source**: Derived from *Foundations of Defensive Leadership*, Soccer Intelligence Journal, 2015.

2. **Vocal Leadership**
- o **Description:** Explains concise commands, encouragement, and signaling danger to maintain team clarity.
    - o **Source**: Adapted from *Communication in Football: The Defender's Role*, 2016.

3. **Composure in High-Pressure Moments**
- o **Description:** Highlights the importance of mental calmness, deep-breathing techniques, and focus drills.
    - o **Source**: Inspired by *Mental Toughness for Defenders*, Sports Psychology Monthly, 2018.

# Annotations and Citations for Chapter 8: Defensive Resilience and Adaptability—Overcoming Challenges on the Field

## Quotes and Insights

1. **Gary Cahill on Composure Under Pressure**
   - **Quote:** "It wasn't just about defending; it was about staying calm when the whole world was watching."
     - **Source**: "Chelsea's Champions League Triumph," UEFA Highlights, 2012.

2. **Chunyi Lin on Calmness**
   - **Quote:** "In the quiet moments of stillness, the greatest truths reveal themselves. Embrace calmness as your guide."
     - **Source**: *Born a Healer: The Quiet Strength Within*, Chunyi Lin, 2007.

3. **Benjamin Pavard's Adaptability**
   - **Description:** Pavard's standout performance at the 2018 World Cup, stepping into an unfamiliar defensive role due to injuries, showcased resilience and adaptability.
     - **Source**: "Pavard's Rise in Russia," FIFA World Cup Archives, 2018.

4. **Porto's Unity Under Mourinho**
   - **Description:** José Mourinho's 2004 Porto team displayed extraordinary defensive unity, staying compact and disciplined to win the Champions League final.
     - **Source**: "Mourinho's Porto: A Masterclass in Defense," Champions League History, 2004.

# Humor and Anecdotes

1. **"Parking the Bus or Driving It Off a Cliff?"**
o **Humor:** A confused defender asked, "Are we parking the bus or driving it off a cliff?!" during a tactical switch.
   o **Source**: Original humor contribution; no external citation needed.

2. **Nervous Midfielder's Nosebleed Joke**
o **Humor:** After filling in as a center-back, a midfielder joked, "I've never been this far back... hope I don't get a nosebleed!"
   o **Source**: Original humor contribution; no external citation needed.

## Visual Aids and Descriptions

1. **Compact Defense with Nine Players**
o Diagram: Illustrates how a defense reorganizes after an injury or red card, emphasizing compactness and discipline.
   o **Label**: "Defending with Nine Men: Compact and Disciplined Defense."
   o **Source**: Adapted from *Strategies for Undermanned Defenses*, Tactical Soccer Insights, 2016.

2. **Responding to Tactical Adjustments**
o **Diagram:** Shows how defenders adjust their shape to counter a formation change, such as an opponent adding a second striker.
   o **Label**: "Adapting to Opponent's Changes: Adjusting Marking Responsibilities."
   o **Source**: Derived from *Flexibility in Modern Defending*, Soccer Intelligence Quarterly, 2017.

3. **Defensive Unity Under Pressure**
o **Illustration:** Depicts defenders maintaining compactness and communicating as the opposition applies pressure.
   o **Label**: "Defensive Unity: Compact and Disciplined Under Pressure."

o   **Source**: Inspired by *Teamwork in Defense: Principles of Compactness*, Coaching Strategies Journal, 2015.

## Lessons and Principles with Examples

1. **Maintaining Composure in Adversity**
   o   **Description:** Highlights the importance of staying calm and sticking to defensive fundamentals, even when facing challenges like red cards or injuries.
      o   **Source**: Derived from *Mental Fortitude in Soccer*, Sports Psychology Monthly, 2014.

2. **Adapting to Tactical Shifts**
   o   **Description:** Discusses how defenders adjust to opponent strategies, emphasizing communication and flexibility.
      o   **Source**: Adapted from *Adapting in Real-Time: Tactical Evolution in Soccer*, 2018.

3. **Trust and Teamwork in Defense**
   o   **Description:** Examines how trust and compactness allow defensive units to weather intense pressure and maintain shape.
      o   **Source**: Inspired by *Unity in Adversity: Lessons from Soccer Defenses*, 2016.

# Annotations and Citations for Chapter 9: Controlling the Game from the Backline—Dictating the Tempo and Pacing the Match

## Quotes and Insights

1. **Carles Puyol on Patience and Control**
   - **Description:** In the 2010 World Cup, Puyol demonstrated the importance of patience, using controlled possession to hold the lead and dictate the game.
       - **Source**: "Spain's Defensive Masterclass," FIFA Archives, 2010.

2. **Franz Beckenbauer on Quick Transitions**
   - **Description:** Beckenbauer, renowned for his quick defensive-to-offensive transitions, showcased how a sudden tempo shift can leave opponents scrambling.
       - **Source**: "Beckenbauer's Legacy: The Kaiser of Football," UEFA Classics, 1998.

3. **Virgil van Dijk on Defensive Command**
   - **Description:** At Liverpool, van Dijk's vocal leadership organizes the defensive line and midfield, ensuring calm and coordinated play.
       - **Source**: "Van Dijk: The Complete Defender," Premier League Chronicles, 2020.

4. **Sergio Ramos on Managing Momentum**
   - **Description:** Ramos's ability to influence momentum through tactical fouls and perfectly timed tackles exemplifies control during chaotic moments.
       - **Source**: "Ramos: Master of Momentum," La Liga Insights, 2019.

5. **Giorgio Chiellini on Balancing Risk and Safety Description:**
   - Known for his "no-nonsense" approach, Chiellini also recognizes when calculated risks can turn defenseinto attack.

o   **Source**: "Chiellini's Defensive Wisdom," Soccer Intelligence Quarterly, 2016.

## Humor and Anecdotes

1. **"Here for Cardio?"**
o   **Humor:** A frustrated defender during a high-pressure match joked, "Are we defending, or just here for cardio?"
  o   **Source**: Original humor contribution; no external citation needed.

## Visual Aids and Descriptions

1. **Tempo Control: When to Slow Down vs. Speed Up**
o   **Diagram:** Illustrates slowing the game by passing back to the keeper versus speeding it up with forward passes into space.
  o   **Label**: "Tempo Control: When to Slow Down vs. Speed Up."
  o   **Source**: Adapted from *Strategic Tempo Shifts in Soccer*, Coaching Dynamics Journal, 2015.

2. **Defensive Communication Tips**
o   **Infographic:** Displays phrases like "Hold the line" and "Watch the runner" to highlight effective communication strategies.
  o   **Label**: "Defensive Communication: Commanding the Backline."
  o   **Source**: Inspired by *Effective Defensive Leadership*, 2017.

3. **Decision-Making Under Pressure**
o   **Flowchart:** Compares decision paths for clearing the ball versus threading a calculated pass forward.
  o   **Label**: "Decision-Making Under Pressure: Weighing Risk vs. Safety."
  o   **Source**: Derived from *Defensive Decision-Making Strategies*, Soccer Analysis Monthly, 2018.

4. **Defensive Resilience Under Pressure**
o **Diagram:** Shows defenders' ideal compact positioning during intense pressure, with arrows indicating recovery and cover movements.
   o **Label**: "Staying Composed Under Pressure: Defensive Resilience in Action."
   o **Source**: Adapted from *Team Compactness Under Fire*, Tactical Soccer Review, 2016.

## Lessons and Principles with Examples

1. **Controlling Tempo**
o **Description:** Explains when to slow the game versus initiating quick transitions, citing Puyol and Beckenbauer's examples.
   o **Source**: Adapted from *Tempo in Defensive Strategy*, 2014.

2. **Leadership Through Communication**
o **Description:** Details the importance of organizing teammates and maintaining defensive shape through vocal cues.
   o **Source**: Inspired by *Communication in Soccer Defense*, 2015.

3. **Decision-Making Under Pressure**
o **Description:** Highlights Chiellini's ability to balance risk and safety, emphasizing the value of sharp decision-making in chaotic moments.
   o **Source:** Derived from *Defensive Instincts: Balancing Risk and Reward*, 2016.

4. **Momentum Management**
o **Description:** Examines Ramos's ability to manage momentum shifts, turning defensive challenges into opportunities for control.
   o **Source:** Inspired by *Momentum in Match Play*, 2018.

# Annotations and Citations for Chapter 10: The Complete Defender—Mastering the Art and Science of Preventing Goals

## Quotes and Insights

1. **Paolo Maldini on Anticipation**
   - **Quote:** "If I have to make a tackle, I've already made a mistake."
     - **Source**: *Maldini: The Art of Defending Without Tackling*, UEFA Magazine, 2005.

2. **Nemanja Vidić on Game Reading**
   - **Description:** Vidić's career emphasized anticipating the game's flow to block passing lanes and neutralize threats before they materialized.
     - **Source**: *Vidić: Reading the Game with Precision*, Premier League Analysis, 2013.

3. **Gary Cahill on Mental Toughness**
   - **Description:** Cahill's performance against Barcelona in the 2012 Champions League showcased resilience and mental focus under immense pressure.
     - **Source**: *Cahill's Iron Wall: Chelsea's Semi-Final Heroics*, Champions League Chronicles, 2012.

4. **Pelé on Mastery and Perseverance**
   - **Quote:** "Success is no accident. It's hard work, perseverance, learning, studying, sacrifice, and most of all, love of what you are doing."
     - **Source**: *Pelé: Reflections on Soccer and Life*, Sports Legends Weekly, 1997.

5. **Descartes on Intentionality**
   - **Quote:** "I think, therefore I am."
     - **Source**: René Descartes, *Meditations on First Philosophy*, 1641.

# Humor and Anecdotes

### 1. Defensive Leadership Humor

o **Humor:** "90% of defensive leadership is yelling 'TRACK BACK!' at midfielders who seem allergic to running. If defenders got paid per shout, they'd all retire as millionaires."

  o **Source**: Original humor contribution; no external citation needed.

## Visual Aids and Descriptions

### 1. Defensive Zones and Key Commands

o **Diagram:** Shows the defensive third divided into zones, with key phrases such as "Mark the runner!" and "Hold the line!" mapped to specific areas.

  o **Label**: "Defensive 3rd Zones."

  o **Source**: Adapted from *Commanding the Defensive Third: A Tactical Guide*, Soccer Strategies Quarterly, 2016.

### 2. Anticipation vs. Reaction Visual

o **Diagram:** Side-by-side comparison of a defender intercepting a pass through anticipation versus being caught flat-footed.

  o **Label**: "Anticipation vs Reaction."

  o **Source**: Derived from *The Anticipatory Defender: Reading the Game*, 2017.

### 3. Steps for a Successful Tackle

o **Flowchart:** Breaks down key elements of a clean and effective tackle, including positioning, timing, execution, and recovery.

  o **Label**: "The Four Essentials of a Clean and Effective Tackle."

  o **Source**: Inspired by *Defensive Fundamentals: Tackling 101*, Coaching Excellence, 2014.

### 4. Defensive Resilience Flowchart

o **Flowchart:** Outlines steps for holding the line under pressure, such as identifying threats, maintaining compact positioning, and reacting to attacks.

- o **Label:** "Decision Flow: Holding the Line Under Pressure."
- o **Source:** Adapted from *Resilience in Defense: Strategies Under Fire*, Tactical Insights Journal, 2015.

5. **Controlling the Tempo Flowchart**
- o **Flowchart:** Illustrates how defenders make decisions to hold possession, clear the ball, or transition to attack based on game situations.
  - o **Label**: "Controlling the Tempo: Balancing Possession and Pressure."
  - o **Source**: Derived from *The Game Manager: Defenders as Playmakers*, 2018.

## Lessons and Principles with Examples

1. **Leadership on the Pitch**
- o **Description:** Highlights vocal commands and the importance of organizing teammates in the defensive third.
  - o **Source**: Inspired by *Leading from the Back: Defensive Command*, Soccer IQ Quarterly, 2017.

2. **Anticipation as a Defensive Superpower**
- o **Description:** Emphasizes reading the game to predict and neutralize threats before they develop.
  - o **Source**: Derived from *Game Intelligence: The Anticipating Defender*, 2019.

3. **Technical Excellence in Tackling**
- o **Description:** Breaks down the mechanics of precise tackling, from positioning to recovery.
  - o **Source**: Adapted from *Tackling with Precision: A Defender's Guide*, Soccer Coaching Weekly, 2014.

4. **Resilience Under Pressure**
- o **Description:** Explores maintaining composure and discipline in high-stakes scenarios, such as defending with a man down.
  - o **Source**: Inspired by *Mental Toughness in Defense*, Sports Psychology Journal, 2016.

5.  **Dictating the Game's Tempo**
- o   **Description:** Discusses controlling the pace of the game through smart decision- making and composure.
    - o   **Source:** Derived from *Tempo Masters: Controlling the Game from the Backline*, 2015.

# Glossary

## Chapter 1: Developing a Winning Mentality in Defense

- **Visualization**: A mental rehearsal technique where players imagine specific scenarios to prepare for match-day challenges.
- **Resilience**: The psychological capacity to recover quickly from setbacks and maintain focus under pressure.
- **Mental Preparation**: Techniques used to build concentration, confidence, and readiness before a match.
- **Goal Setting**: Defining measurable objectives to track progress and performance improvement.
- **Anchor**: A mental or physical cue used by players to refocus during high-pressure moments.

## Chapter 2: Mastering Defensive Positioning and Tactics

- **Zonal Marking**: A defensive strategy where players guard specific areas of the field, ensuring that attackers entering these zones are covered.
- **Man-Marking**: A tactic where a defender is assigned to closely track a specific opponent, minimizing their influence on the game.
- **Hybrid Marking System**: A combination of zonal and man-marking systems, used to control space while targeting key opponents for direct marking.
- **Compactness**: The defensive principle of reducing space between defenders to create a tight, cohesive line that limits attacking opportunities.
- **Anticipation**: The ability to predict the opponent's next move, enabling defenders to position themselves proactively.
- **Offside Trap**: A tactic where defenders step forward simultaneously to catch attackers in an offside position, forcing a turnover.

- **Tracking Back**: When players, especially midfielders, retreat quickly to help the defense after losing possession.
- **Sweeper Role**: A defensive position, often behind the main defensive line, where the player "sweeps" up loose balls or clears threats.
- **Flat Back Four**: A common defensive formation where four defenders maintain a horizontal line across the field.

## Chapter 3: Tackling and Interceptions— The Art of Winning the Ball

- **Front Tackle**: A direct approach to dispossess an opponent head-on.
- **Slide Tackle**: A dramatic move where the defender slides on the ground to intercept the ball, often used as a last resort.
- **Block Tackle**: A technique to absorb the impact of an opponent's movement while reclaiming possession.
- **Interception**: Anticipating and cutting off a pass before it reaches the intended recipient.
- **Jockeying**: Delaying an opponent's progress by positioning oneself between them and the goal without committing to a tackle.
- **Lunge**: A risky tackling maneuver involving a long stride or dive toward the ball, which can result in a foul if mistimed.

## Chapter 4: Working with the Goalkeeper and Defensive Chemistry

- **Pressure**: The act of challenging an opponent with the ball to disrupt their control or decision-making.
- **Cover**: A defender's positioning behind the pressuring teammate to provide immediate backup if needed.
- **Balance**: Maintaining stability in the defensive line to ensure no gaps are left vulnerable to attacks.

- **Trust**: The foundational reliance between defenders and the goalkeeper for effective communication and execution of strategies.
- **Defensive Chemistry**: The synchronization between players to move and act cohesively as a single unit.
- **Sweeper Keeper**: A goalkeeper who actively moves outside the penalty area to intercept through balls and aid in defense.

## Chapter 5: Defending Set Pieces—Mastering High-Pressure Moments

- **Set Piece**: A dead-ball situation, such as a free kick, corner kick, or throw-in, which restarts play.
- **Aerial Duel**: A contest between players for control of the ball in the air.
- **Direct Free Kick**: A free kick where the shooter can strike directly toward the goal.
- **Indirect Free Kick**: A free kick requiring the ball to touch another player before scoring is allowed.
- **Wall**: A line of defending players formed to block a direct free kick.
- **Zonal Defense (Corners)**: Assigning areas to defenders rather than specific players to neutralize threats during corners.
- **Man-Marking (Corners)**: Assigning defenders to tightly track attackers during a corner or free kick.
- **Flick-On**: A subtle redirection of the ball, often by a header, to an oncoming teammate during a set piece.

## Chapter 6: Possession and Transitions—The Power of Scanning and Turning Defense into Attack

- **Scanning**: Observing the field continuously to assess options, threats, and opportunities.
- **Transition**: The tactical switch between defensive and offensive play, often occurring after gaining or losing possession.

- **Counterattack**: A quick offensive maneuver launched immediately after regaining possession, catching opponents unprepared.
- **Ball Retention**: Keeping possession to control the game's tempo and reduce opposition chances.
- **Breaking the Lines**: Passing the ball through defensive or midfield lines to disrupt the opponent's shape.

## Chapter 7: Defensive Leadership and Communication—The Voice That Commands

- **Defensive Leadership**: The ability to organize, inspire, and guide a defensive unit during matches.
- **Communication**: Verbal and non-verbal signals used to coordinate defensive movements and strategies.
- **Vocal Commands**: Clear instructions shouted by defenders or goalkeepers to maintain organization.
- **Anchor Role**: A deep-lying player who provides stability and links defense with midfield.

## Chapter 8: Defensive Resilience and Adaptability

- **Adaptability**: The ability to adjust tactics, positioning, or strategy based on the flow of the game.
- **Mental Toughness**: The resilience and focus required to perform consistently under pressure.
- **Repositioning**: The act of adjusting defensive shape quickly after losing the ball.
- **Compact Shape**: A tight formation minimizing spaces attackers can exploit.

# Chapter 9: Controlling the Game from the Backline—Dictating the Tempo and Pacing the Match

- **Tempo**: The pace at which the game is played, controlled by the team in possession.
- **Game Management**: Using tactics and strategies to maintain control and minimize risks during a match.
- **Pacing**: Adjusting the speed of play to align with a team's strategy or match context.
- **Switch of Play**: A long pass that transfers the ball from one side of the field to the other to exploit space.

# Chapter 10: The Complete Defender—Mastering the Art and Science of Preventing Goals

- **Holistic Defense**: An integrated approach combining physical, tactical, and mental aspects of defending.
- **Tactical Awareness**: Understanding the game's nuances and making decisions based on match situations.
- **Technical Proficiency**: Mastery of the fundamental skills required for effective defending, such as tackling and positioning.
- **Second Ball**: Reacting to and securing the ball after an initial clearance or deflection.

# Mastering Defense: The Art and Science of Preventing Goals in Soccer

## Strategy, Resilience, Perseverance, and the Unsung Heroes of Soccer

*"Attack wins you games, Defense wins you titles."*
*- Sir Alex Ferguson*

# KEVIN LE DOUX

# Mastering Defense: The Art and Science of Preventing Goals in Soccer

## Strategy, Resilience, Perseverance, and the Unsung Heroes of Soccer

*"Attack wins you games, Defense wins you titles."*
*- Sir Alex Ferguson*

## KEVIN LE DOUX